Our Lady of Mile End

Our Lady of Mile End

STORIES BY

Sarah Gilbert

ANVIL PRESS / VANCOUVER

Copyright © 2023 by Sarah Gilbert

All rights reserved. No part of this book may be reproduced by any means without the prior written permission of the publisher, with the exception of brief passages in reviews. Any request for photocopying or other reprographic copying of any part of this book must be directed in writing to Access Copyright: The Canadian Copyright Licensing Agency, Sixty-Nine Yonge Street, Suite 1100, Toronto, Ontario, Canada, M5E 1E5.

Fifth printing: October 2024

Library and Archives Canada Cataloguing in Publication

Title: Our Lady of Mile End : (stories) / Sarah Gilbert.
Names: Gilbert, Sarah, 1967- author.
Description: First edition.
Identifiers: Canadiana 20230455573 | ISBN 9781772142143 (softcover)
Subjects: LCGFT: Short stories.
Classification: LCC PS8563.I4738 O97 2023 | DDC C813/.54—dc23

Cover design: Arizona O'Neill
Interior: HeimatHouse
Author photo: Francis Miquet
Represented in Canada by Publishers Group Canada
Distributed by Raincoast Books

The publisher gratefully acknowledges the financial assistance of the Canada Council for the Arts, the Government of Canada, and the Province of British Columbia through the B.C. Arts Council and the Book Publishing Tax Credit.

Anvil Press Publishers Inc.
P.O. Box 3008, Station Terminal
Vancouver, B.C. V6B 3X5 Canada
www.anvilpress.com

PRINTED AND BOUND IN CANADA

To the neighbourhood
and neighbours everywhere

"If you live in one place long enough, you do not need to seek gossip and rumours; stories, all sorts of tales, will come to find you."

—Yiyun Li, "Kindness" from *Gold Boy, Emerald Girl*

Acknowledgements

To my family, and my family of friends: Paul Bramadat, Merrianne Couture, Helen Evans, Victoria Gilbert, Alyson Grant, Molly Johanson, Joanne Robertson, Connie Barnes Rose, Michelle Syba, Mike Thompson, Maria Schamis Turner, Sabina Walser, Juliet Waters, and Carol Wood.

Thank you, of course, to Amelia and Francis, and Nancy Gilbert, for everything.

Thanks to my students for reminding me of other ways of seeing.

Heartfelt appreciation to Brian Kaufman, Jessica Key, and Karen Green at Anvil Press.

❖

Many of these stories were first published in literary magazines, including *subTerrain*, *Prairie Fire*, and *Taddle Creek*. Thank you to the editors.

The poem "Home" by Warsan Shire appears in full on the website Facing History and Ourselves.

Table of Contents

Material / 9

What If / 19

Our Lady of Mile End / 29

The Three Stages of Boiling / 39

Made in Mile End / 45

Introduction to College English / 57

Banquet / 73

The Letter / 83

The Visit / 95

Something Special / 107

The Sweater / 115

Green Eyes / 127

Picnic / 147

Parade / 155

The Word / 165

Appetite / 181

Catch / 197

Material

Alice didn't love getting naked at work, but for the past two weeks it had been necessary.

The first time, she left her things in a pile on the bathroom floor and was just about to get in when she heard someone coming home and slammed the water off. Yanking her clothes back on, she opened the bathroom door. "Hello?" She walked to the front door of the spacious ground floor apartment, looked in all the rooms. Nothing. No one.

She really needed to wash. The Y had closed for renovations which meant that she and all the other artists who showered there during free swim hours were getting ripe. The warehouses they lived in along the tracks were zoned industrial. No showers or kitchens since you weren't supposed to live there.

Tara was always telling Alice to make herself at home, have a coffee, eat whatever. She said if Alice needed cleaning supplies, or anything at all, to let her know. But Alice hadn't asked about using the shower. Squatting naked, she scrubbed the sides of the tub where it got grubby.

Then she stood under the wide rainfall showerhead and let the water cascade down her back, hot and perfect. It might have been the best shower of her life except the dread of getting caught made her rush to lather and rinse. Afterward, she used her own thin towel and, dressed and dripping, crept from room to room in a tense, backwards sort of hide-and-seek, hoping not to find someone who had arrived while she was under water. Living room, kitchen, little bedroom, empty. In the big bedroom, a figure. She gasped, knees buckling. It was a hanging bathrobe, that's all. It was fine. Completely fine, she thought, pulse pounding. So, she did it again the next week and the week after that. Until, having forgotten her toiletries, she came out of the bathroom smelling like Tara's lavender shampoo and citrus body wash to find her, Tara, standing at the kitchen counter in a belted linen pantsuit, eyebrows raised.

"I was just wrapping up and I took a shower—"

"I forgot my laptop. I thought maybe you were cleaning in there."

"That, too. It's the best way to really get at the sides of the tub." Her sopping hair was a spreading wet spot on the back of her shirt. "I usually shower at the Y because I don't have one. But it's closed."

"You don't have a shower?" Tara studied her, puzzled. "Why didn't you tell me? Next time, just let me know, OK? Avoid surprises."

It was pouring outside, and she insisted on giving Alice a lift, even though she was already wet. The Audi's wipers were on full as Tara rolled up the block to where the neighbourhood dead-ended at the railroad tracks.

"This is me," Alice said. Something was going on. People were milling on the sidewalk among piles of boxes. There was a TV news van and a camera person shooting an interview with a sculptor she knew.

"What's happening?"

"I'm not sure, maybe someone is having an opening or something…" But midday didn't seem like the right time for that. It was as if everyone was moving out, all at once.

Then she saw clear storage bins full of material and the lidded orange buckets from Home Depot, and a stack of canvasses under a thin sheet of clear plastic. "Oh my god, oh my god, my stuff." Alice was out of the car before it stopped moving and ran to where Mac was draping a blue tarp in an attempt to protect it all from the rain.

"What's going on?"

"We got kicked out. The fire department came in and said the place was a fire hazard. They made Stuart open all the doors and I got my stock out and then I grabbed yours. I got your pictures and most of your fluffy stuff and your pails —"

"I have to get in there."

"Can't. They've locked the doors."

Alice looked. The double doors, usually propped open at all hours, were chained and padlocked.

The summer downpour pattered to a drizzle.

"Is this your work? How do you make it? I'd love to take a peek." Tara had double-parked and was looking around, lifting a corner of the tarp to see what was underneath.

Alice was sweating, rendering that shower pointless. If she hadn't taken the shower, she would have finished before Tara had come back for her laptop and Tara wouldn't be here now, poking at her things.

"She paints with found materials," Mac told her.

"I heard," Tara said.

Alice tugged the tarp back down. Loft residents went by carrying crates of art supplies and garbage bags of clothes.

Tara said, "Well, now what? What are you going to do? Do you want a lift?"

"No-yes-thanks-please," said Alice and Mac at the same

time. Mac nudged Alice, motioning to the stacks of her canvases, her buckets and bins, plus his crates of soaps. "We can go to my friend's place. He has room."

Alice had been cleaning their house once a week for months, but they had barely spoken until one day last fall when Tara and Anthony arrived home from work to find her still there, zipping up her backpack, which seemed to be full of their carrots and onions. Tara didn't know much about her, except that she was an artist and had come recommended by their old cleaning lady, a young woman named Elyse, who'd gone to France for a print-making residency. The artists weren't the best cleaners but Tara liked to support them with a steady gig.

"Finally. Is it really you?" Tara joked when they met in her kitchen. "How are things?"

"Pretty good..." The girl seemed to be wondering about the best answer. She was evasive, or maybe just shy, so Tara kept trying. "How is your art going?"

"Well, I'm working on a new project," Alice admitted. "Textiles."

"Great," Tara nodded.

"Actually, I wanted to ask you something."

"You know, friends of ours have a new gallery space in the neighbourhood," Anthony broke in. "They want to give young artists an opportunity because the pandemic has been so hard on creative people. You should get in touch."

"Good idea, Ant."

"Actually, they're looking for someone right now."

"They are?" Tara glanced at him.

"Yeah, remember, they told us they wanted to find

someone to clean their place and the gallery. Would you be interested?"

Alice was quiet.

"We'll give them your number. I'm sure they'd like an arty cleaner. It could lead to other stuff. Foot in the door type thing," he said.

"Nice," Alice said, her tone indicating it was not nice at all. With networking skills like that she'd never get anywhere, Tara thought. Then the girl said, "Would it be OK if I took the lint from your dryer?"

Tara wrinkled her nose. "That's a *textile*?"

Alice waited, her expression blank.

"You want it, go ahead."

"OK, thanks." Alice paused, then added, "What about the vacuum? The stuff that collects in there."

"Yech. Really? What for?"

"I paint with the lint and the dust." She lifted one shoulder and one side of her mouth, as if to say, I'm an artist, all right?

Alice's artwork sounded odd, but Tara wanted to help, especially since she seemed so glum about the possibility of more cleaning jobs. When the girl left with a vacuum bag full of dust Tara felt satisfied by friendliness of the exchange and called, "Good luck! Have fun with your project!"

"She thought I was nuts for asking, I mean, no one wants that stuff," Alice told Mac later. She dished out a bowl of soup and handed it to him. Red lentil and garlic, plus a couple softening carrots and onions that she'd slipped into her bag instead of tossing them into the compost when she'd cleaned Tara's fridge. The slow cooker had transformed the mixture into rich stew. With no kitchen she'd become an expert slow cooker cook.

"You make the soup, I make the soap," Mac said, passing her a matcha green tea body bar. In the studio next door he used his crockpot strictly for cooking up batches of soap that he sold on street corners and craft fairs. "Sure, they think it's ridiculous now. Once you're at the *Biennale* in Venice, everyone will be all lint-positive, dust allies. That's why you ask them, so people will feel like they're part of it: *Yes, that's right,* she used *my* lint, painted with *my* dust."

She batted him with a packet of lint. "Stop."

"No one wants it except for you. That's what makes it interesting. Just don't show them the final product."

"Why not?"

He shrugged. "It won't be what they're expecting."

"I don't think they care enough to have expectations."

The idea had originated with a mistake. At Jasmine's house, Alice had opened the dryer to find a cloud of violet fuzz foaming out of the lint tray. Alice scooped out the airy fluff. What was this stuff and what could she do with it? The culprit: a purple chenille sweater, densely matted and newly tiny. Maybe if she wet it she might stretch it back from doll-like dimensions. She folded it, put everything else away and left the little sweater in the laundry basket. When she received the e-transfer from Jasmine that evening, she hesitated. Was she supposed to refuse payment?

Jasmine was there the next time she went, waiting for an Uber to the airport, surrounded by leather bags and satchels. "I was hoping to see you," she said. "Could you come on Fridays instead?"

Alice nodded, searching Jasmine's expression for irritation. Maybe it was not a well-loved sweater. She always worried about the wrong thing.

Alice's love of old shoe leather, vintage wool blankets and wax candle drippings had landed her in Fiber and Material Practices in art school. Now she experimented, wetting gray dryer fluff and sometimes mixing it with paint or dye and drying it flat on a screen.

She vacuumed the hardwood floors of tastefully furnished triplexes, sucking up detritus of busy lives with soft brush attachments. There were different ones for carpets. She sprayed granite countertops and black glass cooktops with vinegar or cleaner and wiped them to a shine. Then she took pictures. The array of appliances, the wide, flat, living room sofa, the king-sized bed; the closet with lighting that spilled down onto shelves of sweaters.

She'd quit the coffee shop when Elyse offered to hand down her clients. Working alone was better than working with the public. That winter and spring she began to clean for more people, including the gallery couple Anthony had mentioned. "I'm a great cleaner," she reported to Mac.

"Part of your process. Dust for the mill."

"They think it's cleaning. It is my artistic practice."

"Your project offers an implicit critique of our materialist society and our obsession with surfaces. This dust has edge."

She handed him a croissant sliced in thin halves, light as air and golden brown from the toaster. She picked up day-old items, free for the taking at the alley door of the bakery.

"Also, you're a freegan texture freak," Mac added.

"I prefer to say specialist." They munched cucumber and orange slices salvaged from behind the *fruiteries* on Parc Avenue.

Alice decanted the dust from a vacuum bag into a plastic bucket. She had half a dozen pails of it now. Her lint supply had grown into mounds of packets organized in shades ranging from soft pewter to blue to rust. She worked from photos printed out at the pharmacy, first making sketches on canvas which she covered with glue. Then she tweezed threads of lint or sifted dust onto the sticky surface. The dust formed a ghostly background and she painted in oils on top of it to create contrast.

Tara sipped wine from a plastic glass. The gallery was the main floor of Maeve and Eli's big old white castle of a house on the park. She'd left Anthony talking to their friends near the front door. After seeing Alice's life and work tossed to the sidewalk in the summer, she had been the one to describe the situation and encourage Eli and Maeve to consider showing the work of this young person. Tara stopped in front of a wall hung with two paintings. She felt dizzy.

Alice, coming around a corner, practically walked into her. "Tara! You're here."

Tara kept her eyes on the painting. "Now I have a better sense of your work. When you first said dryer lint and vacuum dust, I didn't know how you were going to use the stuff."

"I didn't either, to be honest. At first I thought they were going to be still lifes. The people emerged later."

Tara didn't say anything.

Alice turned toward her and tried to catch her eye. "Maybe I should have asked you..."

"Some warning might have been good," Tara said, eyes still on the picture Alice had painted of them. Because it was them, and, yes, weren't you supposed to ask people, ethically, or at least as a courtesy? There they were in colour, a tapestry-like version of Anthony and Tara, each holding out a teensy cup of coffee to the viewer. Behind them, their countertop espresso machine and the kitchen cabinets were rendered in dusty sepia. Next to this was a companion piece in which all the stainless kitchen appliances were front and centre, thick and dense, weirdly cushioned in various grays of what she assumed was dryer lint, and this time Tara and Anthony were drifting at the edge of the frame.

"The texture is interesting," Tara observed. "I wouldn't have thought of making kitchen surfaces soft but it's kind of, I don't know, domesticating." Clearly, it was a comment on their comfortable life, from someone she'd let into their home and tried to help.

Alice tilted her head as if she were seeing the painting with fresh eyes. Then a journalist interrupted to ask about her process of collecting dust and making something out of it and while little knots of people laughed and chatted Tara moved along to find other familiar faces from the neighbourhood in the work.

The next day Eli called to say most of the paintings had sold. "Apparently people like the idea of having a portrait of themselves in their living room in their living room."

"I'm not sure how I feel about that."

"Feel good," he advised. "Selling is amazing. You might just sell out."

"Not the kitchens," Alice said. "They're spoken for."

There was no answer when she rang the bell at the ground floor of the grey-stone triplex. She let herself in with the key she hadn't used since before the show when she'd taken several weeks off. She carried the paintings through the living room into Tara's kitchen and propped them on two chairs. Alice left her key on the table and let herself out. As her footsteps crunched on the patchy ice, a scrap of pale blue caught her eye. She picked it up, wondering what she could make with the sidewalk's flattened masks, crumpled wrappers and coffee cups.

What If

On a Friday in September, gusts hissed in the leaves outside her window. Meg worked to deadline, while faraway sirens needled closer. She heard a noise in the kitchen and got up to see. Jason was at work and the kids had gone to school. Maybe that squirrel was back. Last week it had come in through the back door. She'd caught it sitting on the table holding a pear in its tiny clawed hands, spitting out the skin into a neat pile.

A man in a gray T-shirt and black jeans was bent over, peering into her refrigerator, his back to her.

"Hey!" Meg said. "What are you doing?"

"Whoa." He whipped around, raising his hands in an *easy now, you got me* gesture. His eyes darted. His shirt was covered with splotches of blue, a messy sort of tie-dye.

"Who—what are you doing here?" she asked again.

"No beer? No pop?" He dismissed the fridgeful of soya milk, oat-milk, almond milk, skim milk, kale smoothie and kombucha with a flick of his hand that also deflected her outrage.

"There's water." This was what she often told Henry and Maude when they complained. Her knees jittered.

The back door had been ajar. He must have thought no one was home. She wondered: do robbers go through the fridge?

His dark eyes jumped to the sink. He turned on the tap and grabbed a glass from her cupboard. She watched his Adam's apple as he glugged one glassful, then another.

As she tried to make sense of the stranger in her kitchen a thought drifted forward from the back of her mind. Could Jason have something to do with this? Was this an actual break-in or some kind of performance?

She crossed her arms and squinted at the intruder who was slowing down on the water. Maybe Jason was testing her with an aggressively interactive piece, like the production he and his theatre department colleagues had staged last year. When people bought tickets, they were cast as protesters, journalists or politicians and expected to contribute to the drama as it unfolded in the halls and stairwells of the university admin building. Breaking the fourth wall destabilized boundaries and encouraged spontaneity, Jason said. Meg said she hated the way that kind of theatre put you on the spot.

Earlier that morning, Jason had asked, "Any plans for tonight?" as he downed his coffee and Meg savoured her last bite of granola, followed by a final gulp of tea.

"Claudia and Sean are coming over for pizza. *Brush your teeth! You have to go, now,*" she called to the kids who'd disappeared.

"We should do something different for once, don't you think?"

Meg had considered this as she ran water in her yogurt-streaked bowl. She looked forward to Friday. She could taste forward to the wine on her tongue; feel forward to the warm floppy slice in her hand, the crisp romaine against her teeth. She could already hear the familiar, almost ritual conversation with their friends, followed by the weekend swimming lessons for the kids, the trips to the library and grocery store, and then the steady rhythm of Monday to Friday again. Routine blanketed everything, true. But mostly that felt comfortable. Comforting.

The stranger tested her boundaries now, saying, "Use your bathroom?"

A theatre type would want to get a reaction out of her. To play along she said, "Be my guest" and stepped out of the kitchen doorway, leaving the way free for him to pass.

He was in there a while. She heard the toilet flush and water run in the sink. Was this part of the play? She walked to her desk and back. She felt uneasy in her own home. Was that the point? An exercise in defamiliarization? Maybe Jason's comment at breakfast about doing something different had been designed to foreshadow the arrival of this stranger.

So annoying. She had a deadline. This was an interruption—a distraction—and classic Jason. He was always provoking her: you need to be less anxious and more playful, he said, less set in your ways, more open to living in the moment.

She called him. Voicemail.

"Hahaha. Very funny. Immersive, taken to the next level. *Our own home!* You got me. Is this what I'm supposed to do while he's in the washroom? Call you? Um, do you think we could go back to tickets and showtimes? Because I have work to do. Call me."

What if this guy was an actual robber? What if he was looking for drugs in the medicine cabinet? There were a few zopiclone, some ibuprofen, and expired anti-inflammatories. If Maude and Henry were home, she'd get this man out, no matter what he might be doing there.

He came out then, the blue still all over his shirt and she saw it was also on his hands.

"That happens to me, too," she said.

"What?" He looked at her with an odd expression on his face.

"Exploding pen?" she nodded at his shirt front.

"Right, yeah," he muttered and lifted his shirt off.

Meg watched him. Abs, ribs and what looked like a home-made tattoo on his bare chest. This display of bone and muscle in her living room was unexpectedly interesting. She discovered she wanted to keep looking.

His eyes had stopped shifting around. "Nice," he said, gesturing at the open, airy living room with the sectional couch, or at her. She wasn't sure. They looked at each other.

Her phone rang.

He put a finger to his lips, conspiratorially. He stuffed his stained T-shirt into his back pocket where it dangled like a flag and pulled on a familiar denim shirt. He must have picked it up in the bathroom.

"What are you talking about?" Jason's voice inquired from the phone. "I got your message. It didn't make any sense."

The stranger went to the kitchen door, paused, turned back, and gave her a jaunty salute as if he were tipping his hat. He bounced down the tight spiral of the fire escape, out the back gate, and into the alley.

"Who *was* that, anyway?" she asked, moving to look out the window, but he was gone.

"What are you talking about?" Jason repeated, exasperated.

"The actor. There was something about him. I'll give you that. Strange, but charismatic."

"I don't understand what you're saying. Why would there be an actor at home this morning?"

"Ha-ha. You're good."

"You keep saying that. I'm not joking."

"That's part of it, right? This conversation is like, the second act?"

"Whatever you say, Meg. I have to go. I'm late for a meeting."

To clear her head, she went for a walk around the block. St. Viateur Street was in chaos. A clutter of police cars was double-parked at all angles. Firetrucks and an ambulance blocked the intersection where a cop directed traffic. As she got closer, she saw that orange cones and yellow crime scene tape surrounded the corner bakery where a car had crashed into the patio. Two more dented cars sat nearby. Everyone had spilled out of the cafés and restaurants and stood on the corner, talking and pointing.

"You missed the drama!" Meg's neighbour, Jasmine, rushed to tell her. "This taxi flew through all the stops, with cops chasing behind, and then the taxi hit a car turning onto St. Urbain and slammed it into the *terrasse*."

The sirens came back to her, the blare penetrating her office.

Jasmine's boyfriend joined them with fresh intel from the café. "The taxi was a getaway car. They held up a bank and stole the cab."

"Those stupid cops! A high-speed chase through the neighbourhood. Excuse me, people live here. Kids are walking home for lunch! What were they thinking?" Jasmine said. "They got out and pulled guns like they were in some kind of movie."

Thank God, Henry and Maude had been eating lunch at school, Meg thought. She walked home and stepped over ruby splinters of taillight lying in the street. Back at her desk she moved words around in her document, deleting and restoring. She tried to focus on her deadline. Control X, control V, control Z.

She clicked on the local news sites.

Two people had robbed a nearby bank, stolen a taxi and sped through the densely populated neighbourhood of Mile End, running stop signs and a red light. The police had chased the taxi until it hit a car, at which point the robbers got out and made a run for it. They caught the woman right away, but the man had run down an alley and disappeared.

Police were asking residents in the area to stay inside, close their windows and lock their doors as canine and tactical units canvassed the streets and alleyways.

People were advised to call 911 immediately if they spotted the suspect, who was known to police.

The bad guy couldn't come into school because they locked the door, according to Henry.

Meg had walked over to pick up the kids after receiving an email from the school saying they weren't allowing children to go home at the end of the day without an adult.

"Why would a grownup want to hide in a school?" wondered Maude who was in grade five. "We'd notice him right away, don't you think? Hey, excuse me, grownup man, what are you doing in my class?"

"Not if he hid in Anne-Marie's closet where she keeps the mops and stuff. Or *le directeur*'s office when he's not there. Or the library room which is usually empty. There are spots, especially if he squinched up tiny," said Henry, who seemed to have considered all the hiding places. "Like in a locker."

Or in somebody's kitchen, Meg thought.

"He was here?" repeated Claudia, her mouth full of chèvre-arugula pizza.

"Right there," Meg pointed at the fridge. The kids were safely mesmerized in front of a movie on the laptop in her office with their cheese and pepperoni. No need to worry them with stories of the intruder.

"Unbelievable," said Sean.

"She thought it was something I'd set up." Jason shook his head, pleased to be credited as the creator of this real-life drama.

"I had no idea what was going on."

"Were you scared?" Claudia asked.

"It gave me the jitters. A stranger in the kitchen. It was weird. And he was covered in blue stuff."

"The ink-pack. I read about that online." Claudia nodded. "Apparently, they only got away with about $400, and it was all contaminated by ink."

Jason snorted. "Losers."

"The bank does that to discourage hold-ups."

"Anyway, I told the cops," Meg said. "They came up and made me go over exactly when he came in and what he did and what he touched. They bagged the water glass and took it with them, just like on TV." She made a face, a sort of shrug with her lips.

"What?" Claudia asked.

"I don't know. As far as I'm concerned, robbing a bank is a victimless crime."

"Oh, come on. Don't go all Stockholm on us here," Jason said. "They drove recklessly and caused a car accident that could have killed someone. He broke and entered our home. He was probably on drugs. Anything could have happened. Don't tell me you feel guilty about reporting him."

"Maybe robbing a bank is not the best critique of twenty-first century capitalism," Sean suggested.

"Did he threaten you?" Claudia asked.

"He drank water and went to the bathroom. Also, he didn't exactly break, he just entered. The back door was open."

"I would have freaked out!"

They polished off the pizza, forked up the wilting remains of the salad, and poured out the last of the wine. Next Friday, Meg thought, she'd get some beer. And pop. "It seemed strange," she said. "I was suspicious."

"Of the wrong person!" Jason pointed out. "Guy got one of my shirts."

Sean nudged him. "It just shows how subversive she thinks you are."

"I think it shows how good Meg's imagination is," said Jason. "It suggests she's secretly dying to do immersive theatre."

"God, no," Meg said. "Not my idiom. I don't even know what to say in real life. Obviously. He was just so—" She had a flash of the man's torso—bare, skinny, wired with muscle, streaked with blue. Instead of experimental theatre her mind wandered somewhere steamier. Turning her thoughts back to her friends and her husband Meg found them looking at her, curious, waiting for her to finish her sentence. She flushed.

"I think he's still at large," Claudia said.

Late that night, Jason went down to the backyard to lock the latch on the fence to the alley. He made sure the kitchen door to the back porch, and all the windows were locked.

Barn door, horse, Meg thought.

He touched her neck and skimmed her ribs and then her thighs with his fingertips as if he were exploring her body for the first time. Meg met him beyond halfway.

"Wow," he said afterward, before drifting off.

The bank robber was arrested on the south shore four days later. The news stories described the noon-hour robbery as a "brazen heist," pulled off with sunglasses, a neck-warmer to hide his nose and mouth, and a cigarette lighter shaped like a gun. The man was reported to be a "career criminal" who had spent years in and out of prison for B&E. The articles said that, convinced of his own intelligence, he often chose to represent himself in court.

Six months after that the pandemic started and hemmed them in with weeks and months that were exact replicas of each other. There was no forward momentum. Meg knew they were lucky, yet COVID dragged on, summer turned to fall, and no one came into the apartment anymore, ever. No friends, and definitely no one different or new. There was no possibility of strangers, no surprise encounters.

That fall, after the incident, before COVID, she would have described her routine as reassuring. Yet sometimes when she was trying to work and having trouble concentrating, she found herself looking out the back door at the fire escape and the alley.

It was not that she worried he'd come back.

More that she knew he wouldn't.

Our Lady of Mile End

When Liette stepped out of work the heat hit her like a soggy sponge. Thick, humid, unbearable—just like it had been that day in 2007. Along Saint-Laurent, people's faces glistened.

Today, customers had complained as Liette scanned their items at the cash, but the air conditioning refrigerated the store so completely that the heat was a rumour she couldn't quite believe. Now, sweat soaked her eyebrows and melted her steps, her sore feet thirsty for the cool garden hose she'd turn on as soon as she got home.

As she walked up the block one of those party bikes loaded with a dozen hooting, pedaling tourists passed her as the speakers sang *"Cel-e-brate good times, come on!"* Liette could make out something in front of her place. Now what? Probably another walking tour in a huddle, as the guide explained how Montreal's outside staircases caught on over a century ago to save space inside. Or maybe it was clothing strewn on a blanket for another pop-up sidewalk sale. Or else her upstairs neighbour, Evan, with his artwork spread out at his feet.

A young woman on her hands and knees was chalking the sidewalk like a kid making a hopscotch. She wore short shorts, and her breasts bubbled out of a bikini top.

"Hey, Liette. You like her?" Evan came out with two tall beer cans and gave one to the girl.

She looked young, like all of grey-haired Evan's girlfriends, but what did Liette care? He was just a neighbour. It took her a minute to realize he was referring to their drawing.

It billowed with waves of hair and arms. A woman held something different in each hand: a glass of coffee, a bagel, a guitar, a laptop, a phone, a beer.

"She's Our Lady of the Coffee," said the girl.

"Our Lady of Mile End," corrected Evan. "Give her your artists hanging by a thread, your trendy young professionals, your gamers, your walking tour groups and tour buses. You've got to admit, she adds some magic to the pavement."

"She adds something, I suppose."

Liette stepped around the squatting girl and through the wrought iron front gate. The ugly white-brick building dated from the eighties, when it took the place of two old triplexes that had burned down. That was long before anyone thought of heritage regulations or cared about how this run-down part of Montreal's Plateau looked. As she turned back to latch the gate she caught Evan rolling his eyes.

She went inside to get away from the artists and their wavy woman. This meant walking right past her coiled hose and the oasis of cool mist she'd pictured for the entire walk home.

It had started that summer, a dozen years ago. Cleaning was the only thing that helped. She'd always kept the front yard tidy, if you could call the uneven stretch of asphalt a yard. But that July was when it had become a ritual. She liked to spray her flowerpots, rinse the paved yard, mist her feet. Watering the pavement calmed her.

When fall came, she raked after work and before bed.

Making piles and bagging them to keep the cracked surface clutter-free quieted her pounding heart. Sometimes, pulse racing, she got up and went out at midnight to pick up the drifting yellow leaves from the Norway maple next door. One by one, she collected every leaf. It helped her almost sleep. The yard spanned the width of the six-plex. On a block where every centimetre was in demand, this space was hers. In the winter, she shovelled it clear and then turned to the broom to brush away the quiet white.

Now she opened every window. No breeze. She doused her face at the sink, peeled off her dress, and laid herself down on the floor underneath the ceiling fan. Not cool enough. She got up and stood in front of the open fridge, wishing again it was possible to store up some of the icy air conditioning from the store and feel it now. It didn't work that way. There was no holding onto anything for later.

Liette looked out the front window. She had to clean the yard before the police showed up. They usually came before the anniversary, and they hadn't been around yet. She had to spray the hose, but Evan and friend were still out there with the chalk, talking and laughing.

She lay back down on the floor, in her underwear, the fan spinning overhead, the rug rough against her back.

The doorbell yanked her awake. Half naked, she tugged on her dress.

A man outside her door pushed aviator sunglasses up onto his bald dome. The rims glinted like the chain inside his white shirt, which was open at the collar.

"Sorry to disturb," he held out a tanned hand, the Ferrari horse prancing on a gold ring. "I'm just here to say hello. We're the new owners. We bought the building from the Carusos."

"We? Who's that?"

He patted the pocket of his chinos.

"I don't have a card with me right now. We'll be doing some renos, but I'm sure we can come up with a good solution for everyone."

Liette looked over his shoulder and saw a large SUV double parked in front. She'd known that Mr. Caruso's kids were selling. Liette, Evan, and their neighbours, all paying seven hundred dollars a month each, would have to go. New owners paid tenants like them to relocate during renovations, then quadrupled the rent.

"We realize a number of you have been here for quite a while."

"Twenty-seven years."

"For you."

He held out a white box.

When her arms stayed at her sides, he set the box down on the steps.

Liette watched the man get in his big car and drive away. No sign of Evan now, of course, when she wanted to know if this new owner had already talked to him. She slipped on her flip-flops and stepped outside, her foot catching the edge of the white box.

The cream filling was dense and sweet, the shell light and crisp. On the front steps, as the sun was setting, Liette ate three cannoli. She wondered if Evan got a box, too. He'd been there about ten years now, arriving a couple summers after it happened.

A minute of misting made the terracotta of the geranium pots give off the smell of wet clay. Robin had shaped her a pottery bowl, in art class, for Mother's Day, in Grade 4. The teachers always got them to do something. He'd been excited, hiding the surprise in his room, putting up a sign—KEEP OUT DON'T LOOK SECRET—and making a big fuss over presenting it, wadded in ten layers of plastic bags, watching her as she opened it, to gauge her amazement. Later, he hid other stuff in his room. There'd been no more signs—none needed. The message had been clear: Keep out. Stay away. That's when she should have gone in. She should have pressed him to talk to her about what he was doing, where he went when he stayed out all night and with whom. Mother's Day always gave her twinges, the displays of flowers, chocolates, and cards reading "TO MOM" in loopy cursive or fake kid writing made her tight heart thump too fast.

Her fingers gripped the lever on the hose nozzle. Today was just as bad, kind of like Mother's Day in July. Where were her annual visitors, anyway? They always showed up to say they hadn't forgotten. If she moved, like Big Car Cannoli had in mind, how would they find her?

Spray caught her feet and felt so good she turned it to mist her torso, legs, face.

Dripping, she loosened her grip so the water turned off as she stooped to picked up cigarette butts. An endless supply blew over from across the street where smokers sat on benches outside the *terrasse* of the café.

"Don't you think it's wasteful, Liette?" Evan had asked more than once. "They say Montreal loses half of its drinkable water through leaks in the infrastructure, and you're spraying the other half on concrete."

She turned it on full and blasted the asphalt.

The water pooled and a trickle ran under the fence,

into the hair of the giant woman they'd drawn all along the sidewalk. Bright water coloured with chalk dust ran off the curb into the street. Tired from the heat, the day, that guy at the door, she watched the colours float.

"Liette! Stop!" Evan banged through the gate and grabbed at the hose. She turned away from him and water sprayed everywhere.

"What the hell? We spent hours on that. Turn it off, you fucking crazy anal bitch!"

Evan took the hose and flung it on the ground. He shoved her shoulder.

"Don't touch me."

"You idiot. You're such a *loser*. Watering the pavement. You're pathetic!"

He jabbed his finger at her sternum, as his girlfriend tried to grab his arm.

Liette stumbled back.

"Get away from me. I'm calling the police."

Still dripping, her flip-flops squelched the cannoli box as she ran for her phone. Damp fingers slid on the screen as she pressed 911.

She looked up from the phone and there they were, filling her doorway. "Already? How—?" The large policemen came into her front hall.

"How are you, Madame Morin? Is there a problem?"

They were here. Their appearance was not miraculous, she realized. They'd been en route, they were here for the other thing.

"Nine one one. Nine one one," the voice on the phone repeated.

"Oh!" she looked at the screen and jammed the red circle to end the call.

"How have you been?" said the older cop, Passard . . . Perreault . . . Tétrault . . . she searched for his name. She had his card somewhere. Silver tinged his temples now. "We understand it's hard. We just want you to know, we're still on it. As we've told you, sometimes the perpetrator of a drug-related shooting is not tracked down for years."

"Twelve, even? Twelve years?"

"It happens, Madame Morin. File's still open. I'm not giving up."

Every year, the same exchange. They knew their lines. What else could they do?

Her phone was ringing. She refused the call. It rang again. She saw it was 911 and thrust the phone at him.

"Community Relations, Officer Tétrault," he answered. "We came to the address for an unrelated visit."

He listened, nodding, and assessed Liette.

"Is anyone in any danger?" he asked her.

She shook her head, wondering why he wanted to know. It was a dozen years too late to do anything about it. Evan's shove came back to her, resurfacing as if floating up from under water.

"Hang on," he said into the phone, gesturing to his colleague who squeezed by Liette in the hall and stepped into each room to have a look around. He came back shaking his head. "Under control," Tétrault said.

Those weren't the words Liette would have chosen as she sat down and looked at their big bodies and giant boots in her living room. The young one was especially big.

"How old are you?" she asked him.

He looked at Tétrault.

"Twenty-eight," he said. He had light hair, shaved close.

They'd moved in when Robin was two. He'd played outside in front. He had a tiny slide. In the summer they filled up a little plastic pool. She was so happy to get a place on the ground floor, even if the yard was paved. At least there was a fenced-in space for him to run around. She kept the stroller inside the front door and the sled for pulling him to daycare in the winter by the steps outside.

"Robin would have been a year older now. I mean, a year older than you. He had big feet too."

The years spun away from her as she spoke. Twenty-seven years here, she'd told the man. Where would she go now? How could she leave? How had she stayed this long? She stared at Tétrault's partner's boots.

They watched her, as if waiting for her to come up with something else. She just kept nodding. That seemed to be all she had to say. Robin would have been twenty-nine. He had big feet, too. He didn't anymore.

"Madame Morin." Tétrault reached out a hand and squeezed her clammy fingers. "I wish you a good evening."

"Wait! Here!" She went to get the dented box. "Take one!"

They looked in and gave her a quick glance.

Liette's T-shirt dress was damp with sweat and water from the hose and it stuck to her body like a wet bathing suit. She looked and saw the pastries in the box had been mashed flat, their creamy guts spilled out of splintered cylinders.

"I suppose they don't look too appetizing anymore—"

Tétrault reached in, scooped up a handful, and popped the goop in his mouth.

"Mmm. Thanks," he said, as if it was the best treat—as good as an ice-cold beer—as if he weren't accepting the loopy offer of a deranged lady. A pathetic fucking crazy anal bitch.

She blinked, tapped the back of her hand to her eyes.

In the dusk, out front, the officers walked past Evan, who said something to them she couldn't quite hear.

Tétrault stopped, spoke to him, gestured to the door where she stood.

Liette held up her hand, a static wave.

She sat down on the steps. Dusk settled over the block. It was still hot. The *terrasse* of the café across the street was quiet except for a few smokers around the outside edges. Most customers were inside now, enjoying the air conditioning. They used to prop the doors open on hot nights, and she'd lie in bed and listen to the clack of balls on the pool table. They got rid of pool years ago, to squeeze in more tables for more coffee drinkers. Young people who worked at the video game company nearby had moved to the area, and families with fancy cars or those bicycles with boxes on the front big enough to carry a couple kids. When the new owners got them out—her and Evan, the Romanian families, and the two old couples upstairs—they would renovate and rent to people like that. Unless they fought it, Liette thought. Maybe in the morning she'd talk to Evan. Whatever the new landlord offered next time he came around, they could refuse it. The tenants could get together, go to the rental board, get legal advice. At least buy some time.

"Liette."

Evan came toward her and then, before he got close, he stopped. His face was blurry in the half dark.

"I didn't know. I mean, I knew about your son, but I didn't know what day it was today. The cop told me. I'm sorry."

The asphalt yard was still damp in spots. Liette got up and walked over to the gate. The girlfriend had a flashlight and was doing touch-ups to their wavy woman with all the arms.

"Maybe you should give her a hose," Liette suggested.

The girl nodded.

"I can add another arm."

"And a shovel."

"Broom?" Evan asked, digging out his own piece of chalk from the pail.

"I think so."

Liette opened the gate and stepped out of her enclosure to get a better look at the woman juggling so many different things.

The Three Stages of Boiling

In the dim store that smelled of raked leaves, the woman behind the counter interrogated Martha. "Is it for you, or is it a gift? Are you a business person? A worker? Or creative? To drink in the morning, afternoon or evening? Stimulating or relaxing? Flavoured or black?"

"Relaxing would be good," Martha replied.

"What kind of pot do you have?"

"A white one?"

"Porcelain," she noted, a generous term for the thick pot with a stained crack running down its side.

She made notes and disappeared behind the black velvet curtain at the back of the store. Martha was left in front, alone. In *The Book of Tea*, Okakura Kakuzo says that Teaism is a cult founded on the adoration of the beautiful among the sordid facts of everyday existence. The Book was a small library book with yellowed pages. It described the five steps for making tea and the three stages of boiling. The first boil occurs when little bubbles like the eyes of fishes swim on the surface. In the second boil the bubbles are crystal beads rolling in a fountain. At the third boil, the billows surge wildly in the kettle. You add the tea at the second boil, at the third you pour in a dipperful of cold water to revive the youth of the water. Eyes of fishes, crystal beads, wild billows. Martha had read The

Book as Gray researched "Vermicomposting vs. Composting" and "Using Earthworm Systems."

The neighbourhood shimmered in a humid haze and the stacks of neighbours in the triplexes on both sides felt suffocating. Gray said it was the humidex. The denser the air, the better sound travels. Martha used to worry about the neighbours hearing them in bed. Now she wondered if they could hear them snapping at each other.

To get away, she'd come to Outremont. Just a short walk to the other side of Parc Avenue, it was a different world. Trees, lawns, parks with trickling fountains. Martha stomped down the cool shady sidewalks. Gray had started it with his carelessness. Sure, she'd yelled, but she'd been startled. Then he'd ratcheted things up by calling her dramatic. She plunked herself down onto a bench by the fountain.

A little girl hopped along the rocks that ringed the water's edge while a pigeon drifted in circles toward the middle of the pond. It made a commotion beating its wings against the water but couldn't move closer to the edge. It was in a flap. Martha wondered if a pigeon could drown. Then a man waded into the water. He grabbed the flailing bird and waded out, depositing it onto the grass and rolling his damp cuffs back down as the wet thing flopped on the lawn. Gray would have done that. If a bird were drowning he would act without worrying whether he could get a disease from a pigeon scratch or how a slimy pond bottom would feel on his feet.

Martha got up and walked through the park. The tea shop on Bernard must be new, or at least she'd never noticed it before. She went down the steps to enter the semi-basement and found two people in quiet conversation. They murmured to each other and ignored her as she touched a cup, a tin, a bamboo tray.

The woman assessed her. She said, "The Tea Master will recommend certain teas for you to choose from, once you have answered questions about who the tea is for, and when it will be drunk. But you'll have to wait until I'm done here." She was solemn and dressed in black.

Martha sat on a wicker chair surrounded by shelves of tiny iron tea pots. Maybe she could use recommendations from a master. She watched as the clerk asked the other customer questions, noted down the answers and disappeared to the back of the store through a black velvet curtain, leaving the two of them alone.

"She gives the Tea Master notes and he searches for inspiration," he told her.

"Really."

"Aroma is so important," he said, as if to include her in an ongoing conversation. "Maybe I feel comfortable standing here with you because your scent is speaking to me in a way we don't even realize. And maybe mine, to you."

There was a moment of silence, as they considered each other.

"I like thinking about this stuff. I'm a sommelier."

Martha bet he'd read *The Book of Tea*. She pictured the sommelier's kitchen. It was spotless. ("One of the first requisites of a tea master is the knowledge of how to sweep, clean, and wash, for there is an art in cleaning and dusting.") Then the tea master's assistant reappeared through the curtain. She looked at what was written on a slip of paper and pulled down one canister after another, holding up the big bins to the sommelier who leaned into the tea.

"Ah, yes" he said, closing his eyes. "Mmmm," as he

inhaled from the next one, and the one after that. The tea clerk sifted different teas into neat packets for him.

The Book of Tea says Teaism is the religion of the art of life. If that's the case, Martha was a heretic, tossing a bag into a cup and adding a splash of milk—sometimes even before it was finished steeping. Such behaviour would scandalize everyone present: the assistant, the sommelier and the Master hidden behind the curtain like the Wizard of Oz.

The Tea Master had now sent a written message. His emissary read it out: "You have a powerful exactitude, you must always remember to save room in your cup for new flavours."

The sommelier listened with his eyes closed, as if he were smelling the words. "Could I take that with me?" he asked.

"I'm sorry," she replied. "It is meant to be ephemeral."

"Of course. Thank you, thank you." The sommelier nodded to each of them and made his way out of the store, home to a kitchen that was certainly perfect smelling and stocked with fine bottles of wine and tins of tea.

After responding to the list of questions, Martha waited alone for suggestions from the Tea Master. It was true that Gray had always smelled good to her. Like sandalwood, for some reason, even though he used no aftershave or lotion or anything. She wished they could go back to that morning, early, to the dappled light coming through the window, to his arm around her as they woke up to the sounds of the neighbourhood.

A few weeks ago, when he had harvested his first batch of castings—that's what you call the compost once the worms have "processed" it—he handed it to her proudly, a loamy little heap on the lid of a yogurt container. "This," he said, "is the Cadillac of composts."

Martha couldn't argue with the principles. Worm composting was more efficient than regular composting because worms turned vegetable matter into soil overnight. And red wrigglers had the ability to turn smelly garbage odourless. But as he'd read to her from the FAQs on vermiculture, digestion is not the only thing worms do efficiently. Red wrigglers multiply faster than rabbits and ten pounds of earthworms can turn into over two tonnes in just two years. "Two tonnes," she reminded him.

This morning, the kids next door had been out back in the tiny yard getting a head-start on yelling and breaking things. She got up, ground some coffee beans, took apart the stove-top espresso pot with a clunk and a rattle. Then she reached down to empty the old coffee grounds into the vermicompost and her hand touched a slimy wriggling mass. The lid of the big rubber tub was covered with a writhing spaghetti of worms.

"Oh my god! Eyew, yuck, gah!" Her surprise made her fling worms onto the floor and counter.

"Don't over-dramatize," Gray said, without looking up.

"That's disgusting. It's out of control."

"*Relax*. It just got too wet in there. Red wrigglers are very sensitive. The conditions have to be just right."

She looked at the pots and pans piled in the sink, dishwater dirty with coffee grounds, last night's dinner dishes stacked on the counter. Scooter parts and bicycle frames sat in one corner of the living room and doors and broken chairs that Gray had scavenged leaned in the hall next to dusty bags of plaster of Paris, saws, spokes, and pails of tools. She decided to go for a walk.

Martha's thoughts were interrupted by the return of the solemn messenger. "The Tea Master recommends a few teas for your consideration. One of them is the Emperor's Blend. Not everyone gets that choice. This, in itself, is an honour," she emphasized. "He suggests that two creative working people in need of peace might deserve this tea." She pulled down a tin and lifted the lid. The shreds of black tea in the cannister surprised her with the smell of clover, hay, a grassy summer field. She found herself murmuring, "Mmmm," just as the sommelier had. The next tin was peppery and pungent, a third more citrusy. The teas were as rich as perfume, they had nothing to do with dusty tea bags. She opted for the transformative powers of the Emperor's Blend; the honoured and out of the ordinary.

By the time she got home it was afternoon. Gray was wiping the counter. The dishes were done, the counter clear, and he opened the cupboard under the sink to reveal the worm tub in its place under the sink, its contents sealed inside; no one was crawling through the air-holes in the lid. Gray rinsed his hands and dried them on a dish towel and hung it up.

Martha put the kettle on. She opened the packet of Emperor's Blend and breathed in the scent of it as she held it out to him. It smelled rich, earthy, slightly smoky, and gave off a hint of something unnamable.

Made in Mile End

At the neighbourhood supermarket, Ruth traded her wheelie bag for a shopping cart. The store had expanded to triple its original size, and now ten times more people came, especially on Saturday.

"Why don't you just go another time, Ma?" Jacob always asked when she complained about weekend aisle jams.

"Saturday is my shopping day."

"You and everybody else. But you could go anytime. Plus, they deliver. You can order on the phone, or even the computer. The guy will bring it up the stairs and everything."

"I like to pick out my own things. I want the nice apples."

"You make it sound like you're going to an orchard. It's Parc Avenue."

"I see those girls who work there filling the carts from someone's list. They have no idea."

That afternoon the dark-eyed young cashier with dimples was laughing with the bag boy at the checkout as she scanned Ruth's items. The manager paced by the boxes of outgoing deliveries, talking on his phone as lines of shoppers snaked back into the aisles. People were piling items onto conveyor belts, paying, filling their cloth bags or knapsacks, and hauling their groceries out of the store. Everyone jostled and bumped against each other and behind Ruth a tall man stood too close.

To get out of there as quickly as possible, she grabbed her receipt and clutched it against her wallet, yanking her wheelie shopping bag behind her. Gusts of wind and bursts of icy drizzle blasted down Parc Avenue as people bustled by with their groceries. A girl in a dark raincoat and fluffy earmuffs came running up to her, waving a five-dollar bill.

"*Madame! Madame!* You dropped this, *Madame!*"

"I don't think so," Ruth said. "I didn't pay cash." Jacob had convinced her to use the card for most things. It saved her trips to the bank machine.

"But it fell from your wallet."

"Not mine." She hunted for her gloves in her purse.

"*Madame*, please."

The clouds were dark. Ice pellets battered their faces. It was no day for standing around arguing about five dollars.

"If you say so," Ruth relented. She took the bill and fumbled to open her wallet without dropping her crumpled gloves.

"Let me help you." The girl flapped her hand in a give-it-here gesture, so Ruth let her hold the wallet while she tugged on gloves and pulled down the earflaps of her cap. Ben would have asked why she was wearing a men's hat. For ear coverage it was the best. The young woman in earmuffs handed Ruth back her wallet.

The pellets turned to rain as Ruth passed the building where she'd worked for a dressmaker back when she first met Ben. She turned off the busy avenue and threaded her way through a clump of people outside the place for yoga togs. Her knee twinged.

In front of the tea store, steam wafted from little paper

cups. The girl holding the tray said the flavour was Birthday Cake Sprinkle. Ruth accepted a cup and took a sip: liquid cherry candy. Tea? At that place they didn't even have normal tea.

She went past the juice bar (smoothies $12) and toward the old garment factory in the Peck Building on St-Lawrence Boulevard. They used to buy Ben's pants there, at Rothstein's on the fourth floor. Now a video game company had the run of the whole six floors. Ruth could see through each building's current facade to what it used to be, but she almost never ran into anyone she knew anymore. "Where did they all go?" she'd wondered aloud to Jacob.

"Ma, they went where old people everywhere go."

"The West Island? Ville St-Laurent? Côte-St-Luc?"

He laughed. "Well, maybe some. But you know…"

"Come on. We're not *all* dead!"

Jacob and his wife, Susie, hadn't gone far. They lived on Mount Royal Avenue in an old factory that had been converted to lofts. Their apartment was all open space, except for the bathroom. When Ruth visited, she wondered when walls had gone out of style.

She parked her loaded bag in front of the lotion store. Inside, little brown jars were stacked on shelves in pyramids.

"Can I help you?" asked a tall young person.

Ruth, feeling short and old, said, "I'm looking for face cream."

The clerk produced a doll-sized tube.

"That's a sample?" Ruth asked.

"It's a small size. We have bigger."

Ruth squinted at the tiny tube. "How much?"

"This one is sixty."

"*Dollars?*" She widened her eyes.

"Clients come from all over the city for it," the clerk informed her.

Back outside, Ruth pumped a blob of grapefruit rind moisturizer from the dispenser affixed to the brick storefront. She helped herself whenever she went by and had always wondered how a store with almost nothing in it survived. Now she knew. The whole area had gone chi-chi. In the summertime, people lined up outside that place on Fairmount for hours to buy a single scoop of salted butter or lychee flavoured ice cream for $6. As she pulled her gloves back on, a group of people in puffy velvet coats trooped around her in search of the tiny tubes of cream. Her hip ached in the damp cold.

She thumped her bulky load up the outdoor stairs one step at a time the way she'd been schlepping groceries for almost sixty years, despite Jacob's talk of her moving somewhere with an elevator.

"*Bonjour Ruth*," called Dominique, stepping out of the door below. She and her business partner had rented the old workroom on the ground floor of Ruth's triplex on the Main, St-Lawrence Boulevard, boul. St-Laurent. Now she bounced up the steps and lifted the groceries to the landing for her, saying, "We're getting everything ready."

"The big day."

"You're coming, aren't you?"

"I'm not wild about parties."

"You have to come! You're a big part of this. Promise me you'll come down for a glass of wine. We need to toast you!"

"I'll come for a drink," Ruth said, still tasting the cherry candy tea as she fished her keys out of her purse.

"*Su-per!*" the young woman said. (*Soo-pair!*).

Ruth wasn't sure she was in the mood for toasting her tenants. The grand opening of the girls' "workshop boutique" made it official: her business was finished.

To Dominique and Sandrine, the place was a museum. "How long have you been here?" they had exclaimed when they first came in and found her stitching a sweatband into a cap on the old black Singer.

Ruth put away her groceries and made a cup of tea. Regular orange pekoe tea bag, splash of milk. After today a handful of people might go up St-Lawrence Boulevard and wonder: that new *atelier*, didn't that used to be something else?

In its seventy-five years as a hat factory, Ruth was sure the place had never seen a crowd like this. She'd spent half her waking hours in there and didn't recognize it. Young people in black sipped wine from jam jars and crunched snacks. Some of the scarred worktables were still in place but the bright fluorescent lights had been replaced by huge balloon-like bulbs that gave off a dim, warm glow. The girls had kept Ruth's old hat blocks and pattern racks and the hand-operated button covering machine ("*C'est tellement* cute, *ça!*"). The old wooden hangers displayed their new creations. Some patchwork pieces had seams showing, as if to draw attention to the handiwork. Many of their clothes looked like uniforms for nurses, or mechanics. Plain, baggy, solid colours, no prints or patterns. Ruth glanced down at the good shirt she'd put on for the party. It was from Simon's, upstairs. Made in China, which she hated to buy, but festooned with maroon flowers. She poured wine into a jam jar and nibbled a square of something shiny and green. Salty paper melted on her tongue.

"*Bonsoir, Madame!*" Sandrine touched Ruth's arm.

"You're here! I was about to go knock on your door," said Dominique, joining them. Ruth watched as Sandrine waved her long bare arms to get everyone's attention while Dominique stepped to the wall and flicked the lights. They both wore what looked like one-piece pantsuits, sleeveless, despite the icy rain outside.

People shuffled and the front door opened for a second, letting in a blast of cool November air and traffic sounds from the street. As Sandrine spoke to the crowd in French, Ruth looked around and spotted a baby sleeping in a buggy, the old style, which was apparently back in fashion. Then there was silence and Ruth realized she hadn't heard a word.

"*Root?*" Sandrine prompted. The French pronunciation of her name made her feel like a carrot or potato.

People turned. They were looking at her.

"You'll say a few words?"

Ruth said, "I make hats, not speeches."

People laughed. Dominique cupped her elbow and led her to the front. Ruth's thoughts zigzagged from the wine and all the eyes on her. She patted her hair, flattened from the cap she'd worn earlier.

She said, "How many of you wear a newsboy, or a flat cap? How about a deerstalker?"

Silence.

"That's right. Not anymore. No one does. You have your own ways." Ruth gestured to a young person wearing a toque with a patch on it that said *WTF*.

People laughed more, although she hadn't meant to be funny.

"I worked here my whole life almost. My husband's family owned this little factory. I promised him I'd keep it going. So, when he died ten years ago, I did. But after a while, the orders dried up. There were just the suppliers, the money pressures, the squeeze—" A lump snuck up and wadded in her throat.

People fidgeted and murmured.

Who wanted to hear about an old lady's dried up concern, she thought. "I'll spare you the gory details. Sandrine and Dominique walked in here one day when I was getting rid of sewing machines. Or trying. Most of them, I couldn't *give* away." Ruth spoke faster to out-pace the lump.

"Now," she waved her arm to encompass the long room, "it's theirs. These girls have big ideas about bringing the *schmata* business back to life in the neighbourhood. My two cents? It's not an easy path. Good thing they're young and strong. I'm just here to say…" there was a pause and shuffling as Ruth searched for a way to tie up the loose threads. "You better buy their clothes! Or else!"

Clinking glasses, followed by clapping. Sandrine raised her glass and said that they were continuing Ruth's tradition of small-scale, sustainable manufacturing in the neighbourhood. "To *Root!*"

Dominique hugged her. People smiled. Some shook her hand as if she'd done something great by going out of business.

"Look at these!" she heard a voice say. She glanced up to see a tall blond woman pointing to the shelf of wooden hat blocks.

"What do you think they're for?" asked her young companion, who looked familiar. It was the clerk from the face cream store.

"They're for shaping caps," Ruth said. "After they're sewn, they're flat. You need to round them out, so they fit the shape of the head."

"Beautiful," murmured the woman, reaching out a long finger to touch the wooden dome that was smooth from years of use. "Don't you want to keep some?"

"They're keeping a few right here. Me, I'm not blocking any more hats."

"They make wonderful sculpture," the woman said, stroking the block again.

So, Ruth took a hat block and put it under her arm. She passed a table of small items and picked up a silky gray camisole. Simple, elegant. She could get it for Susie, Jacob's wife.

At the counter, a young woman with blue lipstick perched on a stool.

"I had it this afternoon," Ruth told her as she flipped through her wallet for her bank card. "I hope I didn't leave it at the store," she muttered, removing all her cards and putting them back in her wallet, one by one. Something tugged at her memory.

"*Madame?* Do you mind?" The girl funneled Ruth, still rifling through her wallet, off to the side to make way for paying customers.

On the phone, the bank wanted her mother's maiden name (Maitland), the name of her first pet (Pickle) and when and where she'd last used her missing card (Parc Avenue).

"I see the charge at the grocery store, $120.58 at 3 o'clock. Then what did you do? Where did you go?" The bank person, whose name was Sabrina, tapped away on her end of the phone, typing her information.

Ruth sat at her kitchen table. "I came home with my things."

Sabrina said, "I see purchases made with your card downtown, including $2,000 at Future Shop and $2,000 more at Sports Experts, along with the maximum cash withdrawal of $800."

Ruth gasped.

"Who do you think had access to your card, Mrs. Fine? Did you ask the cashier at the store for help? Do you think anyone was able to see your Personal Identification Number at that time?"

"Well, I'm not an idiot," Ruth replied.

"Was there anyone there, next to you, or behind you?"

Ruth stopped to recall the busy supermarket, the line-ups and all the jostling. "There was a man standing behind me. Very tall. I couldn't figure out why he was crowding me like that."

"He was probably peeking at your PIN. Shoulder surfing. But he'd have to also get access to your card in order to do anything."

"I just thought he was in a hurry like everybody else in there." All at once Ruth re-saw the whole thing: the young woman outside the store with that five-dollar bill, the tall man standing too close at the checkout. "They were together!" she exclaimed. She told Sabrina everything.

"Don't feel bad. They can be real pros," said Sabrina. "One person gets the PIN and the other one creates contact by asking for directions, money, anything to get the card."

"I *am* an idiot!" Ruth exploded. "I can't believe I let her touch my wallet. That's when she took it. Right under my nose!"

"They target seniors. I'll have to loop in the fraud department now, but it's unlikely the bank will hold you accountable for these charges."

"*Unlikely?*"

Sabrina was gone.

Downstairs at the new shop half an hour earlier, the young woman with the blue lips had turned back to Ruth, who was still searching through her wallet, after the others had paid. "That'll be $111.55, including tax."

"Pardon me?" Ruth had stopped shuffling.

The clerk had shown Ruth the tiny hand-written tag, dangling from a copper-colored thread: "*$97 & tax. Fait à la main à Mile End Montreal.*"

The numbers buzzed in her head. People wouldn't buy her hand-sewn caps (37 operations on each cap and not one straight seam) for $15, but they'd come to the new *atelier boutique* to buy an undershirt for a hundred bucks. Or go around the corner for a sixty-dollar dab of face lotion or a pricey ice cream.

"Do you want to think about it?" Blue Lips had asked.

"I must have misplaced my debit card," she'd told the girl. "I'll come back another time."

Upstairs, at her yellow kitchen table Ruth gazed at the old hat block while on hold for the Fraud Department. Those girls are no dummies, she thought.

They are not idiots. They know what they're doing with their *atelier boutique*. They have to cover costs and finance the whole shebang. Materials, production, and the rent she charged them, which—she now understood—wasn't nearly high enough. They didn't need her good wishes, or for her to urge anyone to buy their work. The young women didn't even need her hundred dollars, which was just as well. They were the ones with good heads for business. She reached out and tapped the smooth noggin-shaped dome.

Introduction to College English

In the darkening late afternoon outside her window at the college, Evelyn saw students move in groups toward bus stops and the metro. She still had twenty more papers to mark. But she had to go pick up Frederique. Five minutes left in her office hours. She capped her purple pen. As she stood to go, there was a knock on her half-open door.

"Come in!" she called, reaching for her glasses.

"Hello, Miss, I mean, uh, *Ms*."

"Maya. Have a seat. I'm glad you came," said Evelyn.

Maya's backpack slid to the floor as she sat down. Powder dusted her smooth cheeks and thick gloss slicked her lips. The slender arc of her eyebrows seemed to be painted on in perfect lines. She kept her phone in her hand. "I wanted to ask you something."

Evelyn jumped in: "I feel like we took a wrong turn last class. I take responsibility for that. I overreacted. I'm sorry. I want you to know it's water under the bridge, for me, at least. For you, too, I hope. Let's move on, clean slate. The rest of the semester is still unwritten, a blank page." She forced herself to stop, scrawling in the mental margins as she spoke: *Avoid clichés!*

Maya nodded, her made-up face unreadable.

Evelyn bobbed her head, too, mind racing. If Maya

were going to file a complaint to the Ombuds Office she wouldn't be here, would she? Evelyn had to take control. Defuse, accept responsibility, and, perhaps, remind the student of her own role in the misunderstanding. "How was your Psych test, anyway?" she asked.

"Good, I think," Maya said. "It was multiple choice."

"What I'd wanted to tell you the other day, is that Katherine Mansfield gives us great psychological insight into her characters, so in a way, reading her work is effective preparation for a Psychology test." Pleased at having brought the conversation around like this, Evelyn took a sip of cold, old tea from her mug.

Maya said, "The test was on the hypothalamus."

Evelyn thunked her cup down on the desk. "I can tell you're in a rush to get through our readings and discussion. I'd just like you to slow down, be open, explore the text more fully. That's your main challenge. Your only challenge, really. You're a perceptive reader with strong opinions."

"Thanks."

Evelyn gave her a look that she hoped was affirming. She patted the arms of her office chair with a concluding motion, and checked her watch: office hours, over. She had to take the bus to Fred's school where the after-care program closed at six. She stood up, bustled her papers into a stack and put her thermos in her satchel. Maya held still, not responding to any of these cues. Sometimes students came into her office with a question they weren't quite sure how to ask, so that took a while. Then, once it was dealt with, they didn't know how to end the meeting. Evelyn had to lead the way. She thought Maya had said she wanted to ask her something, but maybe this was the girl's way of apologizing. Evelyn looked outside. Now it was entirely dark. She said, "Thanks for coming."

Maya pushed a piece of slippery-straight blond hair behind her ear and said, "I need a letter of recommendation." She did not say, '*I'd like to ask…,*' or '*I wondered if…*'; simply, '*I need.*'

Was the student telling her what to do? Evelyn sank back down into her seat, no longer sure of the way out.

Maya sat there, waiting for the frizzy-haired teacher to respond. Her office was dim with just the desk lamp on, and it smelled like cough medicine, it was probably the tea in that sketchy, stained cup. Two days earlier in class, Maya had been busy when Miss Ms. had zeroed in on what she was doing and asked her to read out loud from the course manual.

"I forgot my text," Maya said.

The teacher had walked down the aisle that divided the classroom, scrunching up her bushy eyebrows at the books and notes and phone spread out on the desk. Maya had admitted she was studying for a Psych test.

Miss Ms. nodded, then smiled in her strange way. "I see. That's good. That's *perfect*. We'll come back to that. But in the meantime, put away your phone, and your books for other classes as we turn out thoughts to 'Miss Brill' by Katherine Mansfield."

"Who cares about an old lady who talks to her coat," Maya grumbled.

"Let's unpack that, shall we?" said Miss Ms. "So, why? *Why* should we care about 'Miss Brill'? About this text that was published a hundred years ago. For that matter, why do you think the college requires you to take English?" Her brown-gray hair bobbed loosely in its clip. "Anyone?"

People muttered about learning to write essays and improving their vocabulary and the teacher jotted this on the board.

Outside, branches of gold leaves waved to Maya. The best part of this class was the big windows that gave her something to look at. She said, "To make us read stuff they think is important."

"Why? What do you get out of reading this *'important'* material?" Miss Ms. made a bowl with her hands as if to contain the words.

"I didn't say *I* thought it was important," Maya specified.

"Understood." Miss Ms. scrawled on the board, "Read, quote unquote 'important' stuff.' We'll add quotation marks to indicate it is someone else's idea of 'importance.'" She jabbed air quotes with her fingers (stubby nails, no polish). "You're a natural argumentative writer, Maya. Why else—Justine? Why read literature?"

On the first day the teacher had asked them not to call her Miss. "Call me *Ms.* Wilson, or Evelyn. And let me know what you would like to be called." People said call me Suzanne instead of Xiouxin; say Way, not Whee for Wei; just say Jimmy, forget Dimitri; Isa, please, not Isabelle-Jeanne; and one person, very tall, with a nose ring and cherry-red tips said, in a deep voice, *Justine,* when Miss Ms. called out Justin.

"Literature shows us different points of view," Justine said now.

"Different stories. Different points of view. Thank you!" the teacher wrote this on the board. "It allows us to see the world through someone else's eyes, someone who may be very different from us. Literature can make us feel what it's like to be someone else." She circled POV a bunch of times, squiggled "empathy," and drew arrows to connect the two. Then she turned around and re-clipped her hair, which immediately came loose again.

"We get to know people better in literature than we do in life. Literature gives us access to people's *inner* lives. Their thoughts, pain, mistakes, dreams. I was just reading that the best arguments in the world don't necessarily change a person's mind. The thing that can do that most easily is a good story." The teacher dropped her chalk in the blackboard tray with a click.

What was incredible is that she said this stuff as if they cared, Maya thought as Miss Ms. bumped into the table at the front of the room. Yellow leaves spun down in the breeze outside. It was four in the afternoon and Maya had been up since five. When this class ended, she needed to move fast. She'd been late last week and Simone, who ran the place, had given her a warning.

Maya tried to stay awake and think about the hypothalamus as the scribbled words and arrows swam on the board. Her own writing was clear and neat. In her notes she used yellow to highlight definitions; pink for important quotes; green for homework assignments. Her pages were a wall of colour. Even so, getting up at five meant no amount of highlighter could keep her eyes open after supper.

"What can we tell about Miss Brill and her life from the story?" Miss Ms. was asking.

"She has a boring life," replied the guy in front of Maya. His short hair levelled off in a neat line across the smooth skin of his neck, which reminded her of Daniel, who wasn't responding to her messages.

"What makes you say that, James?"

"She goes to the park and listens to other people's conversations for fun. She's pitiful!" Maya blurted, as James and the others in front turned to glance back at her.

"I think there is something sad here, that's true. Let's take a few minutes to find particular lines in the text that speak to this."

Maya scooted her chair over to look at Justine's text and they spent the next ten minutes searching for lines to prove that Miss Brill was sad, but every sentence they found showed that she was denying sadness. On her phone a text popped up. It was from Emma, who was sitting on the other side of the room: a snoring emoji. Maya sent back a laughing face and checked Instagram where she saw Serena's photos of everyone looking amazing at the weekend party that she, of course, had missed.

Before she'd realized that class-time was perfect for multi-tasking, Maya had sat at the front and one time she'd noticed that Miss Ms. had a sticker, M for Medium, on the pocket of her big baggy shirt for the duration of the class. Maybe once you had gray hair you didn't care, didn't bother looking in the mirror because you just looked old. Maya would definitely dye her hair if it looked like that. Everything about Miss Ms. was messy: clothes, hair, eyebrows, wrinkles, and handwriting.

After a few students shared examples about the old lady at the park, the teacher said, "So, if Miss Brill rejects the idea of sadness, then why does the author bring it up?"

"Just to confuse us," Maya suggested.

"I wouldn't put it like that, exactly, but we could say there is ambiguity. There is happiness with a suggestion of sadness, too. Does that make sense? Don't we often feel more than one emotion at once? What does this suggest about Miss Brill's happiness?"

The teacher often asked more than one question at a time, making it unclear which one they were supposed to be answering. That was confusing and annoying. Again, no one else was saying anything, so Maya replied, "What?"

"We'll come back to that," said Miss Ms., which is what she always said, and it drove Maya crazy. It was practically against her rules to answer a question. All she ever did was ask. And when they gave a bunch of different answers, most of the time she didn't even say which ones were wrong, and Maya knew her classmates in English 101 supplied some wrong answers.

"Right, then," said Miss Ms. "Roberto, what do you think?"

Roberto, at the back of the room with his three-day beard, man-bun, and sweatpants, was smirking at his phone. "Sorry, what was the question?"

Maya sighed. She could be using this valuable time to study. She'd made herself flashcards and hadn't even had the time to look at them.

"Is Miss Brill sad?"

"Yes."

"Why? Can you say more about that?"

"Because she can't get laid."

Roberto's friends in the back row exploded in laughter.

Miss Ms. kept going. "That may be true but how else could we express this idea? We've talked about word choice and college-English appropriate diction. Are you saying, Roberto, that Miss Brill is *lonely*?"

"I guess. Yeah."

"If that's what you mean, it's a good point. How can you tell? Can you point to lines in the text that give you this impression?"

Whatever they said, she wanted lines in the text to prove it. Maya found this tedious. When you're reading, you don't just take it line by line, you read one sentence on top of another on top of another one and get sucked into the whole story. It was aggravating to analyze it to death word by word, she hated that especially when she had so much other work to do. Plus, why keep asking them? What did they know? She was the teacher and she obviously had certain lines of the story in mind so how about telling them what they were so they could move on.

"Miss Brill put up her hand and touched her fur. Dear little thing! It was nice to feel it again..." Roberto read, making it sound as dirty as possible.

"Thank you, Roberto. There is something going on with that fox fur stole, you're right. We'll come back to that. But there's a moment I want to look at first—when Miss Brill feels like part of the performance, part of the concert, the spectacle at the park. Have you ever had a moment like that? Maybe you're listening to music on your headphones on your way home on the metro and all of a sudden you start seeing everything as if it's a movie, and it seems like everyone is moving to the beat and the music has become the soundtrack for your life. Do you know what I mean?"

Maya noticed people around her nodding and thought of how she used to blast music on her headphones and feel like she was at the centre of something beautiful unfolding, back in the day, before she'd had to rush around busy every minute, late for one responsibility after the next.

"She's trying to be happy, despite her loneliness," said Justine in their husky voice.

"Yes!" Miss Ms. responded. "That's a good way of putting it. She is happy, or *trying* to be happy *despite her loneliness*, as you say, and getting swept up in the moment and then—"

"The young people burst her bubble by insulting her," said James, the one in the front with the neatly barbered hair. He probably just had it cut. Maya leaned in to look for any whisper of stray hairs on the crewneck of his T-shirt.

"Exactly!" said Miss Ms., clearly grateful for Justine and James after Roberto. She stretched her arms wide as if she were holding out a giant beach ball to the class and asking them to play with her.

Maya looked at her phone. She really needed this to wrap up. The story was so short, yet it felt like the analysis would never end.

"Who is crying here, when she goes home at the end of the story?" the teacher was asking now.

No one replied.

"I think we all know the answer," Maya sighed. "It just doesn't make sense."

"Interesting point." Miss Ms. nodded causing more wisps to fall from her hair clip. "Can anyone elaborate?"

James offered, "It says she heard something crying. But she's alone except for her fox fur, which is a dead animal, even though she talks to it like some kind of pet, which is creepy. So, she's really the one crying. It's like she just doesn't want to admit it."

"Very well said! You're zeroing in on the crux of the story here." But then, instead of telling them the point, she just came up with another bunch of questions: "What is the narrative point of view of the story?" she asked. "And how does it affect our understanding of this character?"

Maya wanted to scream. She tapped her screen and read out loud from her phone: *"Miss Brill is written in third-person limited omniscient. This allows us both to share Miss Brill's perceptions and to recognize that those perceptions are highly romanticized."*

"Sorry?" Miss Ms. looked surprised. "What was that—Maya?"

Maya read the explanation again. Miss Ms.'s face seemed to change shape. She was silent for a minute, then said, "What's the point, Maya?"

"You tell me, Ms."

"Let me guess. Study.com? Schmoop? Essay 123?"

"This is from Wikipedia."

"So, tell me. What's the point of sitting in class and looking shit up on the internet?"

Miss Ms. had said *shit*. Everyone stared. Even the students who'd been quietly texting, stopped. The teacher's face was getting redder and her eyes were wide and slightly wild. What's her problem? Maya thought. Roberto was the one who had talked about the old lady getting laid, or not. Maya wasn't the one who'd departed from college English diction. She glanced down at a text from Emma: "Uh-oh. Look what u did!" It was always interesting when a teacher lost it but best when you weren't the trigger, that way you got to take in the show without worrying that you'd caused a heart-attack. There was an old teacher she'd heard about who'd taught a class, gone to his office, and died.

"Why bother with English class at all?" Miss Ms. asked now.

Because it was a required course. Because they had no choice. Maya decided not to make these points at the moment.

"What is the point of post-secondary education, anyway?" Miss Ms. asked. "Why bother? Why not just stay home on your fucking phones and look shit up?" She put her chalk down on the table where it rolled off, hit the floor and broke into pieces.

"To…discuss?" Justine suggested.

Miss Ms. nodded and swallowed. "I'm sorry. I have to… I'll be—" She walked out of the room.

They all sat in the classroom and wondered what to do. It was as if the bus driver had left the vehicle in the middle of the street and walked away. Were they supposed to wait, or get out? Across the room Emma raised her eyebrows and looked at Maya, who shrugged.

If she left right now, she could arrive early for once, a nice change from having to race down to the metro and back up and then run some more. It wasn't her fault if Miss Ms. lost it. Phones exist. Also, internet. Besides, unlike half the people in the room, Maya had been paying attention. Now everyone was taking this unexpected break as an opportunity to look openly at their phones, instead of sneaking looks while pretending not to. Irony.

After what seemed like ages with no driver, Miss Ms. returned. Her face was shiny and puffy with droopy pockets under her eyes and her hair was worse than before. That's why she wanted them to care about Miss

Brill. Miss Ms. was a sad, lonely old lady herself. She pushed her glasses up her nose.

"I'm sorry," she said. "Maya, I apologize for my outburst." The teacher stood still. No pacing around or knocking into things.

"I was actually just trying to answer the question," Maya said.

Miss Ms. gave a slow nod. "The thing is, when I ask a question, I want you to think about it and try answering yourselves. We're here to engage with the literature and with each other. That's the difference between class and looking up answers on your phone." This time she did not swear. She stacked up her papers and books and turned her back on the class. The engagement was over, apparently. Maya and the other students left the room as Miss Ms. erased the board in big swipes, clearing it of words and squiggles.

Evelyn glanced at the girl in her office. Outside, cars' red tail lights flashed. She was late now but she needed to be careful.

"It's for a scholarship through the community centre in my neighbourhood," Maya told her, fishing in her backpack, pulling out a brochure, slightly crumpled, and handing it over. "You're always saying I have good ideas and questions, so…If I apply now, I can get it for next semester."

Evelyn pretended to study the paper. In her mind she scrolled through images of Maya. Maya doing homework for another course in class; Maya leaving thirty minutes early; Maya using her phone instead of thinking; Evelyn losing her mind. Maya asking for a favour. The girl clearly thought she had something on her after that wreck of a class the other day.

Maybe she did.

Evelyn took a breath and set the leaflet down on her desk. Was Evelyn being manipulated? Maybe she was just getting paranoid. Maya was bright and determined. Oppositional? Comes with the territory. How wrong was it to openly look up information on a text in class, anyway? Rather than demonstrating the value of discussion in addition to internet answers, Evelyn had bungled the whole thing and started swearing. A colleague had once told her, *They're just looking for reasons to think you're an asshole. Don't give them any.*

Maya looked around as she waited to see if the teacher would recommend her. In the low light she peered at the photos tacked up on the bulletin board over the desk. She'd made arrangements and for once she wasn't in a hurry. She noticed a photo of a little kid in a yellow raincoat. The kid appeared in many pictures at different ages, sometimes with the teacher and sometimes with the teacher and an old guy, the two of them together with a baby, then a little girl—wait. Could that be? Maya looked at the teacher. Did Miss Ms. have a family?

Was it possible that Miss Ms. was not the solitary English teacher in the story? Did she have a kid, at her age? That might explain the wrinkled clothes. Maya noticed some of the old moms at the park looked practically like homeless people. Never mind that, the other day in the college bathroom after class Maya had spotted a big blobby streak of dried yogurt on the front of her best Adidas hoodie. She thought of Miss Brill and her disgusting fox fur. Maybe they were all going around with some messed up idea of how great they looked.

The teacher looked at the clock on her computer and jumped up, blurting, "I'm late! I have to go."

"OK, right." Maya recognized the urgency and backed out of the office, squeezing her binder into her bag. "Sorry. Thanks, I mean, if—well, bye."

Evelyn picked up her satchel, pulled on her jacket, clicked off the desk lamp and speed-walked down the fluorescent-lit hall, empty now. After all that, Maya had rushed out without waiting for an answer. Noticing her bag was too light, Evelyn jogged back to her office to collect the stack of unfinished—never finished—papers to grade. As she stepped into the dark room her foot sent something skittering across the floor. She flicked the light on. Something must have fallen from Maya's backpack. She bent down and picked it up. One of those small bowls with a lid on it. The kind that kept the Cheerios inside until a little hand poked through the star-shaped opening and grabbed some. Every mom of a toddler had one.

Evelyn paused.

In light of new evidence, she reviewed the images: Maya checking her phone obsessively; Maya using class time for other homework; Maya leaving class early, in a rush.

Evelyn held the bowl up to her nose and inhaled: Cheerio dust.

To whom it may concern,

I am writing to recommend Maya Robitaille for the Community Scholarship for college studies.

As a student in my Introduction to College English class, Maya sparks lively discussions in class. Her impatience to learn as much as possible as quickly as possible keeps me on my toes.

I know that she keeps up with the readings and assignments in her other courses in addition to mine. It is also clear to me that she is determined to balance her academic commitments with her responsibilities outside of school.

If you require further information, please let me know.

Ms. Evelyn Wilson
Department of English

After "Miss Brill" by Katherine Mansfield, 1920

Banquet

An artist Bri recognized, her hair streaked with silver, took the mic, and intoned names: "Louise Malenfant, Dan Bernard, Mike Wood, Laurent Dutaud, Guillaume Robert, Zoey Laframboise, Anna Mark…" The artist continued, standing in front of a vacant storefront's dirty window while a guitar player punctuated each name with a minor chord.

"The evicted," a man near her said to the woman next to him. "Amazing there's anyone left."

Bri felt a flutter in her chest. The recitation continued. Strum-strum-strum-strum went the guitar. She half-expected to hear her own name. Months ago, the new owner of the rowhouse where she rented the basement apartment had told her to look for a new place. She'd told no one. Saying it aloud would have made it real. She put it in a far cupboard in the back of her mind so she could be free to enjoy every drop of summer in the neighbourhood—her neighbourhood—and its slow drift into fall.

She watched two young women in polka-dot dresses meet two sweet-faced guys with Dutch-style bicycles and wander off together. Mothers pushed double-decker strollers loaded with tiers of babies. A Hassidic man hurried by.

Although the day was golden, Brigitte was glad she

had decided to wear her leather jacket. The maple on her street, always the first one to turn, glowed rosy at the top and a slight chill rose from the pavement. Bri put up a hand and touched her collar. She had taken the jacket out of the closet that afternoon, rubbed the dry black leather with vinegar and linseed oil to bring it back to life. "What the hell took you so long?" it seemed to ask. The lining was ripped. "Never mind, tough guy, I'll sew you up later," she'd murmured. It was like an old friend. She touched a zippered pocket, rolled her shoulders back under the weight of the leather. She felt a tingling in her hands and arms. When she breathed, something light and sad—no, not sad, exactly—something fluttery seemed to move in her chest.

Bernard Street was closed to cars and the loose crowd of people milled around in the street and stood on the words that had been painted on the ground in giant yellow letters: *NOSTALGIE*; ANGER; *ESPOIR;* SOLUTIONS? ADAPTATION?" The neighbourhood citizens' committee was hosting this community potluck as a response to the flurry of commercial and residential evictions. They called it *le banquet des résistants*. Yes! Bri had thought when she saw the poster. Not just a block party or a potluck, but a banquet. Someone was singing with the guitar now, in front of the empty storefront. One developer had been buying up properties, forcing out the small businesses by tripling the rent, then leaving the spaces empty until someone with deep pockets came along, usually a chain. A banner rippled in the breeze: *MILE END IS DEAD. THANKS FOR YOUR BUSINESS*.

The song wound down to applause. Bri stood on her tiptoes to glimpse the head of the neighbourhood committee who spoke for a few minutes, then shouted, "We need strict new regulations from the city! No more evictions! Fight speculation!" He raised a fist and stepped aside. She should talk to him. Get advice, she thought as she took a seat at her usual spot. The city councillor spoke next. His hair was thinner and whiter, his body bulkier than on the campaign posters. He said the city wanted to support the residents in their efforts to preserve the unique aspects of the area.

Bri shared her bench with a couple: a man with wispy hair and a plump woman in a batik skirt stared ahead without speaking. Too bad. Bri always looked forward to overhearing conversations. She had become expert at listening as though she didn't listen, at sitting in other people's lives just for a minute while they talked around her.

Perhaps they would leave soon. This morning had been disappointing, too. Outside the café, a couple in their early thirties, he in fastidiously white sneakers and black sweatpants and she in Lululemon, had sat down with their lattes. The man had gone on about which washing machine they should buy. The woman had nodded in agreement to everything—stackable, Energy Star, online reviews. But it wasn't enough, because the man said to the woman's shrugs, "Why do I even bother? You don't care." Bri, bored by the couple and jealous of their budget, had wanted to tell them, 'Be happy you can afford appliances.' It seemed everyone except her had their own machines now. The grungy laundromat was often empty.

People stopped to talk, some twisting open beers. Little children swooped around laughing; she spotted her neighbour's six-year-old, Henry, in a satin dress and a Batman mask and cape. Some kids she didn't recognize at first because they'd changed size and shape over the summer. The adults Bri had been seeing around for years, too, were changing. The moms were faded, beakier, the dads, thicker. The skinny professor with salt and pepper hair walked by with her greyhound, chatting to the guy who scavenged scrap metal for his sculptures in the vacant lot along the train tracks.

"Good crowd," the sculptor observed.

"I thought there'd be more," Professor Greyhound replied.

These two were older, rumpled, and looked as though they'd excavated their long-sleeved fall clothes from deep inside the closet and gotten dressed in the dark.

Slender branches shimmered yellow above the sidewalk and the blue sky paled as late afternoon turned to evening. People sat at picnic tables in the street, eating and sharing plates of tomato and basil, asparagus quiche, flung-open boxes of pizza. A teenaged girl proffered a platter of home-made cookies. A man held out a dish of kielbasa chunks speared with toothpicks. Toddlers clutched plastic bowls of crackers. There were babies in pouches, slings, and buggies. Men with bushy beards, long shorts and tattooed calves leaned on propped up skateboards. Some people drank wine they'd brought from home in stemmed glasses.

Bri loved the banquet, just like she loved the spring soil and plant giveaway; the Italian marching band and spaghetti dinner of San Marziale on the first weekend of July; the late September Art Parade. At the Halloween and winter solstice lantern processions she carried her mason jar lit with a glowing candle inside. She attended the basement bazaars at St-Michael's—the cabbage-smelling variety put on by the Polish congregation, and the arty ones run by hipsters. She was part of it all. No doubt somebody would have noticed if she hadn't come this evening. "Where's Bri, anyway?" one café regular might ask another. She used to go to the café in the morning and Taverna at night, before it moved to the other side of the tracks and the original location turned younger, trendier. She'd been in this village of urban streets since she first got her BA and found her basement apartment on a quiet street. The rent had been cheap back then and had only gone up a small amount every year. Her coordination job at the dubbing company came with free passes to movies and film festivals and a steady pay cheque, which had seemed more than ample after years of part-time student jobs.

At her corner café, when she'd first seen local actors and film production people, she felt triumphant. She had landed far from the small Ontario town where she'd grown up. She had a degree! A cultural job! An apartment in Montreal! She fell in love and made a vow to the neighbourhood. It was only now, at forty-five, after two decades had passed and caused strange shifts around her, that she wondered if she'd miscalculated. The poet next door she'd once dated had stopped to say hi a couple summers ago, when he, his girlfriend and their child were pedaling to their place in Rosemont. The neighbourhood photographer she'd been involved with had moved to the other side of town with a woman and her teenage sons. And this evening, she glimpsed her musician ex-boyfriend at the edge of the crowd, a toddler on his shoulders. A former fixture at the café with her, he now held hands with his much younger wife, who appeared to be on the verge of giving birth again at any moment. "Wow!" Bri mouthed.

She waved to show how happy she was. Happy to see him, happy to see *them*, happy with her choices in general—and specifically right this minute.

She'd packed up her container of black beluga lentils, her fork, and a single beer and put on her jacket. The lentils had turned a disappointing muddy brown when cooked, and she could see now that her food was all wrong anyway. She should have brought something easy to share, like empanadas, or pizza, or crinkly triangles of spanakopita.

Her friend Ana, a dancer and yoga teacher who'd moved back to Peterborough, compared life in the neighbourhood to a sitcom where they all had their parts to play. That's why Bri always made sure to leave at the same time when she went out for her morning coffee. She didn't want to come in late and disappoint the others. It was performance, of course. She put on lipstick, fixed her hair, her jacket. Not everyone would understand. Maybe that's why she felt shy about telling people at work when they inquired, "Good weekend?"

"Yes, yes," she always said. "I hung out in my neighbourhood."

What if she'd said, "Actually, I'm doing this improvisational-sitcom-project."

"Really?" they would ask. "You are?"

And Bri would pat her desk and look down and say shyly, "It's something I've been doing for a long time."

Now she felt a clench of panic in her gut. What if she lost her part?

She had asked around discreetly and checked the online listings. She'd stopped to read all the posters on poles for lost cats, bands, stolen bikes, and yard sales, in the hope of spotting an apartment share or sublet or transfer of lease. A small affordable place? Not around here. Not anymore.

The musicians had been taking a break. They started again and played something warm, sunny, yet there was just a faint chill—a something, what was it?—not sadness—no, not sadness—a something that made you want to sing. Bri saw a writer—a one-time regular at the café—she hadn't glimpsed in years. He'd grown *old*. Over the years, many familiar faces had just evaporated. There'd been people she used to see at the café all the time, even on Christmas morning. They were the people who had no family close by and nowhere special to be. Mario, the café-owner, gave them all a Christmas shot of brandy in their coffee. They were the ones who'd been here since the beginning, or at least since the '90s. That's what today's event was about. How to hold on: how to stop the change that had already happened. The new people, the young families with down-payment money from parents, careers in medicine, videogame design, or who-knew-what. The people who bought a duplex and dug out the basement and opened up the back with windows and added a mezzanine on top to create a single-family monster home—in her village. There were a few of Bri's people left and some, like the wrinkled old writer with the tattered shoulder-bag, had come back for this. A reunion!

The music lifted, the setting sun shone; and it seemed to Bri that in another moment all of them, the whole street, would burst into song. The young people, laughing and moving together, they would begin. And then she too, and the others on the benches—they would come in with a kind of accompaniment—something low, that scarcely rose or fell, something so beautiful—moving. They were all in this together. Bri's eyes filled with tears and she looked smilingly at all the people she'd been seeing for years on the street and lined up at the pharmacy and in the aisles of the grocery store and in the slow lane of the pool at the Parc Avenue Y in bathing caps and swimsuits. Yes, we understand, *we understand*, she thought—though what they understood she didn't know.

Just at that moment a young couple came and sat down next to her. They were beautiful. The girl held out her phone to get a selfie of their heads together, faces glowing, long limbs entwined. And still soundlessly singing, still with a trembling smile, Bri prepared to listen.

"Don't," said the girl. "Come on."

"Why not? Her?" asked the guy. Bri touched her neck casually, looking around to see who he meant. "Who cares? Who gives a shit what *she* thinks?"

"Her *jacket*," giggled the girl. "So *retro*. So '80s. Not in a good way. She's wearing, like, a whole dead cow. And she thinks it's legit."

"Whatever," said the boy in a bored whisper. "Come here—"

"Not now. Not here. I'm starving," said the girl, standing up. "I wonder if they have anything vegan."

On Bri's way home on a Saturday night she usually got a chocolate bar, a good dark one, at the grocery or the pharmacy. It was her weekend treat. Sometimes she tried a new kind: pink peppercorn; cardamom; chili pepper; grapefruit. If she'd never tasted it before, it was like carrying home a tiny present—a surprise. She hurried on those nights and filled the kettle for herbal tea with an added flourish.

But this evening she passed the stores, the untouched bottle of beer clunking against the glass container—still full of lentils—in her bag as her footsteps struck the sidewalk. She went down the stairs into her dark little closet of an apartment—a closet that wasn't even hers anymore—and sat down on her red duvet. She sat there for a long time. She unzipped the jacket and without looking, threw it in the corner. But when she turned her back, she thought she heard someone crying.

The Letter

Frederique locked the door behind her and zipped her cat-shaped keychain into her pocket. Purr-fect, read the tiny printing. October morning chilled her wrist. She tugged her sleeve down and, out of habit, glanced up at the apartment window. Empty, no waving parent.

"No growing while I'm gone, Frederique. Can we agree on that?" her mom had said before leaving to get the train, her kiss warm on the part in Fred's hair.

Red-orange maple leaves feathered down as *The Order of the Phoenix* thunked in her backpack. It was the longest Harry Potter. Her dad had left early for work, bike tail light blinking, and with Mom away the apartment felt hollow. She read about the Defense against the Dark Arts to forget the lonely ache in her stomach. Now she had to run.

The gray tabby slipped out from behind the tree and Fred bent to stroke its dusty back. Harry had Hedwig; she would choose a cat, like Hermione. A skateboard thrummed down the sidewalk and the tabby darted. "You're going to be late!" Theo said, rolling by.

"Come back!" Fred called to the cat and stepped into the street to peer under the parked cars.

A voice came from somewhere low to the ground. "You looking for Tortuga?"

Fred saw frayed pantlegs and wool socks. The guy in the droopy clothes was sitting on the curb with his usual beer in a bag, even though it was eight in the morning. Sometimes he leaned in doorways by the Mission, across the street from school. He wore socks with no shoes.

"That's your cat?" she said.

"She's a special one." The guy had a soft voice and sleepy eyes. "I'm Nestor. What's your name?"

In books the people who noticed children and animals turned out to be magic. In real life, they were homeless. Serge, who slept on a cardboard mat outside the grocery store, bowed to Fred when her mom gave him a loonie. Jeanne, by the bank machine, gave her winks and high fives. Back in kindergarten, Fred had lined up with her classmates at the window to watch a guy who'd come over from the Mission. Pee arced from his penis into the school's bushes. After that the school had put up a fence to protect the strip of green. The fence kept out the Mission people and the kindergarteners.

Fred looked up the block. A deep quiet enveloped the street, as if every kid had disappeared forever. The bell had rung.

"Do you want to be my friend?" Nestor asked.

She ran.

At recess Fred went to the bench with her *Harry Potter*. In the sun it was warm enough to sit still and read. But Lola got there first, with Lenore.

"Excuse me, we're talking *privately*," Lenore informed her and Lola just shrugged, as if she had no say in this, as if she and Fred had never been friends in every other grade until Lola had moved and started walking to school from the other direction. Fred moved to a spot at the edge of the playground where she read about Harry's discovery of the prophecy.

In gym they were doing Circus Arts so they juggled scarves that floated, almost magically, in slow motion. At 3:30, the sky was turquoise with cotton ball clouds. Breezy sun took turns with silver gray gloom. Fred held the book against her chest and slung her backpack over one shoulder. She kicked through drifts of sun-toasted leaves on the sidewalk and stopped at the cedar hedge to watch the sparrows puff into fluffy spheres.

"That one's scary." Theo hopped off his board and nodded at her book.

"I've read it before," Fred said.

"What's going on in there?" He looked into the bushes.

"Sparrow orchestra."

"They're like little balls. Noisy ones. You eleven yet?"

She shook her head. Theo, grade six, was a year ahead of her. He was part-orphan because of his mom. The adventures in books always started when the parents died. But Theo's life didn't seem full of adventure; he sometimes just smelled like a face cloth that needed to go in the laundry.

"When's your birthday?" he asked.

"Two days after Halloween."

"Well, let me know what happens, Fredo." He put one foot back on his board and started to roll.

"I thought you'd read it."

"To you, I mean. When you turn *eleven*."

Theo knew. He was right. She was waiting for the letter, although she pretended, even to herself, she wasn't. She hugged the book. There was no actual Hogwarts, and no magic and therefore no invitation to go study at the wizarding academy would arrive for her by owl. But still, she ached for magic in her life. It was ridiculous. She knew that. A cold wind pushed clouds in front of the sun and the birds bobbed on their twigs.

"You like animals, huh? Fredo? That your name?" The guy, Nestor, had appeared out of nowhere.

Maybe he'd been there all day, watching cats and sparrows. Fred noticed Nestor's socks had a layer of grime on the bottom.

"I want to show you something." He padded into a yard full of broken chairs, white buckets and old window box planters. He went to the front door and opened it. So he had a home, but no shoes. "You like cats, right? What if I said, babies?"

Fred took a step closer. Kittens? she thought. An old tabby was nice, kittens were irresistible.

Nestor had his hand on the doorknob. "You coming?"

Fred hesitated. The clouds had piled up and turned a heavy gray. Her dad wouldn't be home yet.

"Come on." Nestor went inside.

Almost every apartment in every row house on the street had a long hall with rooms blooming off both sides and a kitchen at the back. But Fred knew you could never really tell what someone else's house was like until you got inside and smelled it. Cigarettes and cat pee. Dark walls, hot radiators.

"Right this way, *mademoiselle*." Nestor went ahead.

Way back in the dim kitchen at the end of the hall, heaps of dark clothes were piled on the table. Open cat food cans covered the countertop and stove and filled the sink, as if Tortuga was the only one there who ever ate. Fred couldn't breathe. She was sweating in her fleece.

Nestor lifted the latch to open the door to the back porch and motioned to her. Inside a bin full of rags there was a bunch of furry ovals: kittens the size of hot dog buns. Gray, orange, white with spots. Tortuga jumped in and they wriggled toward her.

"How old are they?" Fred whispered.

"A few days, maybe a week. Go ahead, touch one."

"I don't know." Was it bad to pick up super tiny kittens or baby birds? Did it make them smell wrong to the mother? What if she wouldn't feed them?

"They don't mind," Nestor insisted.

"I don't want to hurt them—"

"Don't worry about it." His hot breath hit her face. "You want to, don't you?"

She did. She reached out and brushed her finger against the pale tannish-orange one. The babies formed a fuzzy row and burrowed into Tortuga, who curved around them.

"You love animals. Me, too." He picked up the kitten and held it out to her.

Fred put down her book so she could hold the tiny scoop of life, as light and warm in her palms as a fresh bagel. If her dad weren't allergic, she could get a cat. Its eyes were tiny slits.

Nestor jostled around beside her. "Look."

She glanced at him and then back at the kitchen and the long dark hall between her and the street.

Nestor had something in his hand. "Look," he said again. "Look at me." Nestor's soft voice was bossy. Did he have another kitten? She felt the orange one, dandelion soft in her hands.

If her mother were home, working at her desk as usual, when Fred came inside she'd say, "There you are. Where were you? I was starting to wonder." That's what she always said when Fred dawdled extra minutes. Today, no one would notice.

She looked. Nestor was pulling on it, not a kitten. Fred had seen her dad's, and the Mission guy's outside school, but Nestor's was a different shape. His hand was moving and he watched her. His stare was connecting it to her.

She didn't want to look; couldn't stop looking. At school, a social worker had come and told them it's not necessarily total strangers. It could be an adult you know who asks you to do something you don't want. It could be friends of your family, or coaches or neighbours. Nestor was a stranger-neighbour.

There was a noise from the kitchen behind him. "Nestor?" A voice called. "What are you doing?"

"Nothing!" Nestor fumbled.

"Who is it? Who are you talking to?"

"No one. No one, Ma!"

An old woman clomped out to the porch with a cane. Her straight white hair spiked out from her head in all directions and her face was wrinkled like used tissue paper.

Fred plopped the kitten in the bin and pushed open the porch door to the yard. Every house had a backyard onto the alley. Tall weeds in the yard brushed her legs as she banged open the rusty gate and ran for it. Down the alley through the fallen leaves below the high bare branches, she ran toward the back of the church on the corner, running until she hit a soccer ball that bounced into her path.

"Hey, pass it here!"

Theo was kicking the ball behind his place.

She gave the soccer ball a running kick and ran past him until she got to the end of the alley and the church steps.

Her watch said 4:30. Her dad still wasn't home and her mom wouldn't be back for days.

Theo came up with his ball and rested his foot on it. "Want to play?"

Fred looked at him.

"What?" he said.

"The guy."

"What guy?"

"The *guy*. With the socks?"

"My dad says not to talk to him," Theo said.

"He showed me his kittens."

"It'd be so fun to have a kitten. Our cat is *old*." Theo passed the soccer ball from one foot to the other.

"He wanted me to touch one. They were tiny." Fred shifted on the concrete steps and let her knapsack slide off her shoulder.

"Did you hold one?"

"He undid his pants."

"What?"

"You know. He took it out."

"What?" Theo said, again. He squinted at her, picked up his soccer ball and sat down on the steps.

"What? What? What?" Her laughs fizzed out like pop from a shook-up bottle.

"It's not funny, Fred. What happened?"

"His mom came and I ran away."

"We have to tell someone."

"My dad's not home yet."

"Mine either."

"My mom's away." She shouldn't have said that to Theo whose mom wasn't coming back. She blinked a few times and reached for her bag. It felt light. Empty. Her stomach dropped.

"My book!"

"What about it?"

"I left it. I left it there." She'd put it down to hold the kitten. She could see it on the floor, on that porch.

"It doesn't matter."

"But—"

"Come on," Theo gave her shoulder a light tap with his fist. "I'll lend you mine."

His house was the same as the rest, a hall with a kitchen at the back. At Theo's the walls had been knocked down so the kitchen and living room were one big space. He got out a bag of cereal, dumped some in two bowls and handed her a carton of soya milk. "It'll make you feel better if you eat something."

"Are you lactose intolerant?" Fred asked.

"My dad. Sometimes we get oat milk. Or almond."

She took a bite. It was the same cereal they had at home. The kind in big bags that was so crunchy when she ate it for breakfast it drowned out her parents.

A black cat stalked in. All its stuffing had leaked out somehow, leaving it bony. "Mrow."

"Hi Hopper," Theo said, between bites. "He's eighteen. We have to give him fluids."

"What do you mean?" Fred reached down. When she took care of the neighbour's cat, she had to put a tiny cat aspirin inside a treat. Hopper's spine was bumpy. His fur stood up; cat bedhead. He rubbed against her shin and purred.

"This." Theo showed her a pouch of what looked like water. "Subcutaneous solution. He hates it."

Fred spooned more cereal. If she were at home she'd be eating cookies with the reading lamp on. It was starting to get dark out. Hopper settled onto a magazine lying open on the tabletop by her bowl. She petted his side.

"You can help me give Hop his stuff. First, I have to warm it up." Theo put the pouch of liquid in a big bowl in the sink and turned on the tap. "When it's ready, you keep petting his head so he won't move. I'll hook him up."

"What is it?"

"It's sodium and stuff to hydrate him. I have to inject it under his skin."

Theo plucked up the loose skin between Hopper's shoulders and stuck the big needle in. The water ran from the bag down into a tube to the needle and into the cat. "His kidneys aren't working anymore. It's good you're here. That means Dad won't have to do it. He makes up excuses not to."

"Really?"

"Hopper was Mom's cat when they first met. Dad says Hop was her first baby. It takes a couple minutes. Look, he likes you. He's not even trying to move."

Fred stroked Hopper's head and the cat closed his eyes. After another minute Theo took the needle out, smooth as a nurse. Hopper stayed still under Fred's hand. He was skin and bones, except for a pocket of water under his fur where he'd been pumped with liquid. Theo said it would spread out. Hopper stretched and jumped down. "Thanks for helping me," Theo said.

Fred was about to leave when Theo went to get something. He handed her the book. "I made it *disapparate* from where you left it and *apparate* here. It's yours."

"Yeah, right."

"Keep it."

No one gave their Harry Potter books away, not even her babysitter who was twenty. "Just until I get another one," Fred said. She tucked the big book into her bag and stepped out into the cool fall evening, steadied by its weight.

Fred had to talk to a policewoman who asked her to get in the front of the car and point out Nestor's house as she drove slowly up the street. The principal emailed all the parents, advising them to walk their children to and from school or else get them to buddy up, due to an incident in which a certain individual lured a student inside with the promise of kittens and then exposed himself.

Theo and Fred walked to and from school together. By the time Fred's mom came home it was as if she'd been gone for months.

Halloween arrived with the usual throngs of kids packing their street in the dark and some houses played music and sound effects from speakers, with parents in costumes and makeup, offering clouds of candy floss and cartons of popcorn. Fred dressed up as a cat, making a tail out of a coat hanger and black duct tape and sticking ears on a hairband. Two days later, it was her birthday. There was a family party with cousins and cake.

Then one gray leafless day in November, she got home and found a plump envelope on the floor where it had come through the mail slot. It had her name on the front and *Hogwarts* written on the back in spidery script with a star next to it. There was a little drawing, of a bony black cat labelled *Hopper Potter*, that made her smile. It wasn't until she held the letter that Fred felt a pang. Her hope for magic to arrive seemed like something from a long time ago. She had stopped waiting for it.

The Visit

Evelyn was incommunicado. After a sweaty bike ride, she'd gone wading in the golden shallows at the beach. Minnows grazed her shins, and, bending over to peer at them—plop. Her phone dropped into the river, lying underwater on the mica-flecked sand just long enough to get wet deep inside.

Now it was on the cabin porch drying out.

She pedalled into town to call Marc from the payphone outside the post office. He was working in the city, and Frederique was with him, taking advantage of the Wi-Fi. Evelyn stopped at the store and picked up milk, bananas, beer and potato chips, and biked home with a full basket.

Every time she sat down to work, she thought of other, more urgent things to do. She'd heard you were supposed to put every distracting thought on a list to think about later:

- Replace phone?
- Get new plan?
- Get Wi-Fi @ cabin?
- Reasons not to get Wi-Fi @ cabin
- Call Mom
- Call Georgia

Turned out the only thing she was writing was that list.

On the fifth morning of solitude, her dead phone rang, startling her mid-toast.

"Hey, I'm in your time zone, just heading home now. Thought I'd call." It was her brother Dominic, calling to say hello/goodbye.

"You're so sentimental." Evelyn's voice cracked like an old person's. It had been days since she'd spoken to anyone.

"I know, I know."

"It's good to hear from you, Dom."

"Yeah well," he exhaled. "I've been on the road for over a week."

"Good trip?"

"Should be. Heading for a multi-million-dollar sale up at the mine in Val d'Or. If all goes well, a whopping commission will be coming my way."

"Multiple millions, huh?"

"Not all for me, sadly. Heavy equipment is expensive."

"It doesn't grow on trees?"

He laughed. "What's new with you?"

"Spending some time at the cabin. Super green, quiet, except for the birds. Hey," she felt the idea form as she spoke it. "It's been ages. Why don't you come visit me?"

In the pause she heard him blow out a lungful of smoke. "That'd be nice and all, but I really can't. I need to get home. My bed's calling me. My cats. My very own bottle of bourbon."

"I have a spare bed. I may even have a bottle of bourbon. It's a beautiful day. Change your flight," she urged. "We can relax, go for a walk. You've never been here. Come see."

The sun was still behind the trees, edging up in the sky. Mist hung in pockets between the maples and the pine grove. Hammocks of spiderweb clung to the grass, cradling dew, and the air smelled of the wild strawberries that dotted the grass. A hummingbird hovered until another zoomed in to fight for the spot at the feeder.

The Laurentian road ribboned up and down, past lakes and through tiny towns before Google Maps told Dominic to turn off onto a gravel drive that curved around a meadow. He gunned the rental car up a steep incline and pulled into a clearing at the top of the hill. Sun shone on a poppy patch near a weathered but tidy log cabin. He realized he'd been bracing himself for a fly-infested shack in a muddy swamp. A screen door opened, and a skinny person stepped out. Was that middle-aged woman with streaks of gray his kid sister? Christ.

He grabbed his smokes and stepped out of the car, knees creaking, back aching. "Hey, kid. Big change from the city. Definitely more parking here."

"Yeah, that's why I like it. Good parking spot." She shook her head at him, smiling.

He grinned. He'd never understood how she could stand living where all the houses were squished together, and people parked bumper to bumper. The streets and sidewalks were busy with people, her place was sweltering in the summer and drafty in the winter. The toilet was in a closet off the kitchen, instead of a decent shower you had to squat in the tub holding a bendy hose, and the wires running from the neighbours' rooftops to the hydro poles looked like something out of a favela in Rio. At least here there was room to breathe. He lit a cigarette.

"Nice poppies." The bright tissue petals bowed in the sun. He waved his hand in front of his face. "Too bad about the blackflies."

"They're on the wane now." She walked around the cabin to a porch that looked over the valley.

"Where is everyone?" he asked. She'd said she was alone but there was always a chance her child or husband might show up. If he had to be sociable, he'd regret the detour.

"Marc has to work. And Fred thinks Netflix is more fun than being here with me, go figure."

"That kid *is* more fun when you're not around," he said. Something about the way Evelyn acted with her daughter made each of them too much, as if no one had ever had, or been, an only child before.

Evelyn looked at him like she was about to say something, and then changed her mind. Instead, she held the screen door open and gestured inside like it was a grand hall. "We've got the whole place to ourselves."

"Whoo-hoo!" He put out his half-smoked cigarette on the sole of his boot and tucked it in the pack, which he slipped back into his shirt pocket. The cottage was just one room with steep stairs up to what he guessed were a couple of bedrooms. Flimsy cabinets lined a wall in the kitchen corner. The floor was parquet buckling in the humidity and a lumpy couch sat in the corner by a woodstove. But there were windows on all sides that let in the dappled green of the surrounding forest. He watched as she ran water and spooned coffee into one of those stovetop espresso pots.

The leafy breeze outside reminded him of their childhood home where he'd let her play his records and taught her how to make scrambled eggs and grilled cheese just right. He said, "Speaking of having the place to ourselves, remember when the parents came home during my eighteenth birthday bash?"

"Yeah, yeah, I know. And I told them, first thing, Dom and Tina used your bed, but it's OK, they changed the sheets." Evelyn shook her head. "I think I wanted attention. Like, '*Hello, parents. You deserted me.*' I was only nine. I woke up in the night and there were teenagers all over the house, the yard, and even across the alley in the park. Not even Georgia, the responsible big sister, was in control. The party was still winding down when Mom and Dad came home the next day."

"Amazing I thought to do the laundry, actually. That must have been Tina's idea. *Tempus* sure does *fugit*."

A woodpecker tap-tap-tapped on the outside of the cabin, as if counting off the years.

"Eventually I had my own party when they were out of town and I had to call you for help." She handed him a chipped teacup of coffee and went out to the porch where there was an IKEA patio table with two hard little folding chairs.

He squinted at her. "You did?"

"You came over and glared at people, remember? They left."

"Saved the day, huh. Comes in handy having an asshole for a big brother."

"Well, I knew you had experience."

"Yeah, I've got some practice at being an asshole."

"With *parties*." She knocked his shoulder.

He took a sip and winced. "Your coffee is going to kill me."

"You're the one who doesn't take milk. I could add water to turn it into an *allongé*."

"Nah, I'm a regular coffee kind of guy." Dominic pushed the cup away.

Evelyn couldn't quite believe it. Had her brother really come to visit her? To make the most of their day she decided they'd walk to the river. She grabbed a water bottle, some sunscreen and put a few snacks in a bag. On the way, they stopped to visit the graves in the little cemetery where a dozen valley residents had been buried the century before. Red-winged blackbirds perched on a wire. Bright yellow finches flitted from the pines. Dom said, "I love goldfinches."

"I never knew you liked poppies *or* goldfinches."

"There's probably a lot you don't know about me."

A note in his voice caught her by surprise. Despite his thick cranky crust there was something tender-hearted about him. "So, tell me something then," she said.

"Ooof. Kind of hard to start now, don't you think? We haven't lived in the same city in what, thirty-five years?"

"Yeah, but we come from the same mix, the same batch of dough," she said.

"I suppose."

She bent down to touch the lichen-covered grave markers flush against the grass: *Mother. Father.* The stone letters were rough against her fingertips. "Might as well set me straight. You came all the way out here, right?"

"Nice to finally get an invitation."

"Oh, give me a break." She squeezed out of the gap in the cemetery fence and walked along the road, her heels sending stones scattering.

Evelyn walked by the old schoolhouse, kept on past the deserted farmhouse and then followed the route of the old railroad tracks that had been turned into a cycling path along the creek to the river. It was midday now and hot. Shadeless. Her feet crunched on the gravel. Cows dotted the soft green hill beyond the blue barn.

Dom walked so far behind her she wasn't sure he was still there. She slowed down. Eventually he caught up and said, "You didn't tell me we were going to walk twenty miles."

She turned to glance back at his feet. Black leather, pull-on boots, with a low heel and his bootcut Levi's over them. Not exactly summer footwear. The same motorcycle boots he'd always worn, even though his motorcycle was long gone. "Not much further. Blisters?"

He shrugged away the question along with her offer of water and lit a cigarette.

A heron rose from the creek in slow prehistoric flaps.

"Tell me about your girls," she said. "How are they doing?"

"Not speaking to me, so I don't know."

"Come on, Dom."

"I call, they don't pick up. I text, they don't reply. What am I supposed to do?"

"I don't know. Show up?" she suggested. "Ring a doorbell?"

"That's a little scary. For me, I mean."

"Don't be a weenie. Don't you miss them?"

"I'd rather it didn't turn into a decades-long Cold War, yeah." He paused to watch goldfinches flutter in a tree near a stretch of wild raspberry brambles.

"Especially since you're on the other side of the wall now. Dominic, you've been through this kind of thing with Dad. But you're the adult this time. You've got to grow up."

"Maybe I'm a double agent," he mused. His chuckles rat-a-tat-tatted, woodpecker-style.

"Oooh," they both gasped at the same moment as an indigo bunting dipped between trees like an iridescent blue sparrow.

"How's Emily doing?" she asked him.

"Not sure. I know she was part of a show at a gallery and I missed it."

"Why didn't you go?"

"I was travelling and then I was tired, and I was busy with work, and I thought I had more time to check it out, but it ended before I got there."

"Uh-oh."

"I apologized. More than once. As far as she's concerned it's just the proof she needed: I'm an inveterate jerk."

The path dipped into the cedar-smelling shade and then reached the old railway bridge. Upstream, the rapids churned white before the river curved and smoothed out along a wide bend of golden sand.

"Welcome to our beach."

"Nice." He lit a cigarette and leaned over the railing. They looked down at the water moving.

"A true jerk wouldn't have rescued me from high school," Evelyn told him.

Back when he still rode the motorcycle that went with the boots, he used to pick her up and whisk her away. She held on to his back, he accelerated, and high school disappeared.

They walked down to the beach and skipped stones where the river slowed.

"Aren't you hot?"

He stood in the sand in his jeans and boots, face red, sleeves rolled up. He looked hot. Not in a good way.

She stepped out of her sandals, rolled up her shorts as high as possible and waded in. This is how she'd dropped the phone but now she had nothing in her shirt pocket.

He patted his for smokes.

Dominic's back was killing him after that walk and he had a headache, probably from the undrinkable coffee and not eating anything all day. His heels were bleeding.

When he got up from a nap, he picked mint from the garden, dissolved sugar into simple syrup on the stove, and, with a bottle of bourbon he found on top of her cupboard, made mint juleps. "You should get a real fridge," he remarked. "And these ice cube trays are from what—1979?"

"It's the *cabin*. It's not supposed to be state of the art."

He worked at finding a comfortable position on the sagging couch. "Have you ever tried sitting on this thing? You need a hammock. And how about *one* goddamn comfortable chair."

"It's true," she said.

"What's that?"

"You do act like an asshole."

He smiled, raised his glass in her direction.

"Maybe it started out of contempt for your family members. Like, if we're stupid enough to believe the asshole act, we deserve to have a jerk for a brother, father, son." She looked at him. "That way you can be mad at us for not understanding you, and you get to feel hurt and superior at the same time."

"I'm not sure I'd put it like that. But if you say so."

He watched Evelyn swirl the crushed ice in her glass and gulp the minty-sweet tea-coloured drink. He realized his sister was tipsy.

She blurted, "Fred is afraid of you, you know, from that time you snapped at her for using your iPad. You also barked at her for not eating the food at the restaurant and snapped when she recited her school project for you in French."

"Well, I don't speak French. Or understand it."

"Not the point."

"She shouldn't be scared. I'm not so bad."

"I know it, but Fredo doesn't. Why do you have to be like that?"

"I thought you had all the answers," he said.

"Well, I do think it's become a habit. And it's hostile. Besides, it's BORING." She took a swig of her drink.

"Well, ex-cuse me. I never meant to bore you," he laughed. She was already a little beyond tipsy.

"Please try to be less predictable."

"Got any books I can read?" he asked. "A thriller set in WWII, or something about the Stasi or the KGB, maybe with a hammer and sickle embossed on the cover? Your stuff is tough for me."

"My stuff?"

"You know, all those heart-breaking short stories. That one where the guy pawns his watch to buy her combs for her hair and meanwhile, she's cut off her hair to buy him a watch chain…I can't take it!"

"What, 'The Gift of the Magi' makes you misty?"

"I want to bawl my eyes out," he admitted.

"Are you for real?"

"Why do you think I act so tough?"

She gave him a collection of stories by a writer whose bio said he'd put himself through school working as a logger and a miner.

Slim pickings ingredients-wise but he made a marinade for the chicken and some dough for naan, then sat on the porch outside, smoking, while he grilled everything on her rickety Canadian Tire barbecue. She washed the grit off garden lettuce for a salad.

"This is delicious," she said, folding the soft naan into her mouth.

"Next time you come we can explore the old gold mine up the road," she suggested. "It used to be open for visits."

"If you want to explore a gold mine, you should come up with me next time I go to Val d'Or."

"Road trip. OK, why not?"

After dinner, they sat in chairs on the grass in the inky dark. He polished off the bourbon. They looked up at the sprinkle of glinting pinpoints until their necks hurt. In the distance the river rapids rumbled like a highway.

"Too much description, not enough plot," he told her the next morning, handing back the book.

She knocked coffee grounds into the compost bucket.

"I'll try it again someday when I'm not so tired." He stepped outside. She brought a cup to him on the porch where he was smoking. He took a tiny sip.

"Would you like some breakfast? Toast? Multi-grain cereal?"

He shuddered. "I don't touch the stuff." He put the cup down.

She followed him to the car, dew damp on her toes. "Thanks for coming. Next time I'm home I'll come out to your place. I owe you a visit now."

"Maybe we'll even change the sheets for you," he replied.

Evelyn shook out her hand, stiff from scrawling in her spiral-bound notebook, and stood up. She heard the wood thrush that sang in long tuneful bursts in the half-hour just past sunset when the day was dissolving. It was the loneliest moment.

At least, he'd made the effort to come and visit her out here in the country. They had walked and talked and looked at birds, cooked out, and drunk bourbon.

That is, they might have. If she'd invited him. If she'd pleaded and managed to convince him that it would be worth it.

In real life there'd been no call from the airport. He'd emailed, mentioning back pain from what he'd thought was a ruptured disc. At emergency they'd given him anti-inflammatories, and an appointment for an eventual MRI. But a month later, in agony, he drove himself back to the hospital. He never left. A scan revealed cancer everywhere. This was back in the early days of the pandemic. No one was travelling. She didn't get out there, two provinces over, to see him. Three weeks later, he was gone.

Out on the porch, she picked up her phone and tapped the black screen. Nothing. Inside, she plugged it in again. All dark. It would not come back to life.

The last light faded from the sky.

— for Bart

Something Special

In the Laurentians where they'd rented a cottage to get away from the busy corner, the days were an early summer medley of leaf green and lake green. Martha and Gray swam in the clear deep lake, diving off the dock and surfacing in bubbly swirls. They made sandwiches for each other, scooped big bowls of ice cream, cracked open beers. They lounged on the deck with a view of the glinting lake through the trees.

While Gray read, Martha walked the gravel road around the lake, exploring. Iridescent dragonflies flitted, snapping up the last few blackflies. Early in the week she met a gold dog who bounded down a driveway and from then on accompanied her on all her walks. Sometimes a young family in a minivan drove by, or a guy in the dusty red Fiat from the end of the road. The drivers waved, as people do in the country. After that, when she saw the mom unloading groceries in the driveway, or Mr. Fiat picking up his mail at the bank of mailboxes, they exchanged sunny hellos. Martha collected wildflowers. When she looked them up in her Peterson Field Guide, they turned out to have names like cow vetch and bladderwort and they shriveled immediately. She noticed a huge thick-stalked plant called cow parsnip that grew over six feet high all along the road. Like Triffids poised to take over the world, Martha thought, imagining an edge of menace in the summer air.

At dusk when the mosquitoes came out, she and Gray went inside and flipped through stacks of old *National Geographics*. "Was that a hoot or a wail?" Gray asked at the first loon call.

"A yodel or a tremolo," Martha suggested, as a different lonely warble echoed the lake. The loon book divided the calls more precisely than they could.

Martha picked out a DVD from a stack on a shelf. "Look, *Dirty Dancing*!"

"You don't want to pollute the lake with that."

"Oh, but I do." It was her favourite plot. Klutzy girl turns svelte dancer overnight. What could be more satisfying? Martha inserted the DVD and pressed Play.

"Why is her name Baby?" Gray wanted to know.

"Be quiet!"

Johnny used a mossy log over a stream in the woods to coach Baby on balance and a cushion of lake water to teach her to jump fearlessly into his arms. "Yeah, right," Gray murmured, but he didn't leave the room.

"She learns to dance like a pro in a week," Martha sighed.

When it was over, Gray pulled her up from the couch. "Wanna dance?" They swayed together. It was not like in the movie, although they did end up undressing in the living room and moving naked into the bedroom as a pale green moth the size of a sparrow fluttered by the window screen. Crickets sang and bullfrogs groaned. Vacation was a canoe sliding across the glassy lake.

On the longest day of the year, Martha shut the fridge and stepped out onto the deck. "We should drink that champagne tonight. Where is it?"

Gray stopped reading and put his book over his face, blocking her out along with the sun. "Whereswhat?" His voice was muffled.

"The famous champagne. I reminded you to pack it."

"Oh. There's a little problem," he muttered.

"What's that?"

"I didn't pack it."

"What? Why not?"

No answer.

"Huh?" she lifted the book off his face and uncovered a guilty smirk.

"It's gone. I drank it."

She stared at him, amazed.

"When you were away."

"What are you talking about? We were saving it for a special occasion!" She waved his book in her hand.

"It's just champagne. It doesn't matter."

"But we were *saving* it," she repeated. "I can't believe you drank it *without* me." She dropped his book onto his chest, felt a heavy thud of knowing. "It was that person, wasn't it? I went home to visit my family over the holidays and you cracked open the fancy champagne with a *stranger*."

"It was spontaneous, I told you. I met her Christmas Day—we were the only people at the Laundromat. It was so depressing."

"But you *chose* to be depressed at Christmas. You *like* that."

"It was nothing," Gray repeated, hardening.

"It was *not* nothing. You could have had nothing, but instead you had champagne! The whole point of champagne is that it's special which is why you pulled it out. It was a gift to both of us and you drank it with some coked-up circus gymnast!"

"Oh, don't get all psycho."

"I'm not *psycho!*" she shouted.

The spur-of-the-moment dinner with the Cirque de Soleil trapeze artist had come up back in January. He mentioned it like he had nothing to hide. It was impromptu, a coincidence of timing. Martha was annoyed at the time, if he'd wanted to celebrate the season, he could have come home with her, the reason for him to stay behind had been to work and avoid festivities.

"I bet you didn't drink it warm. How spontaneous is chilling a bottle of champagne?" she asked now.

"I can't believe you're making a big deal out of this."

She threw a magazine at him.

The thick blue bottle had been a gift from friends who'd brought it back from France. Actual *champagne*, from Champagne. Not prosecco or cava or vin mousseux. The real thing. They'd had it for over a year and had been saving it up for just the right moment, or so she thought. Martha felt retroactively betrayed and freshly irritated by Gray and this acrobat. Instead of the festive summer solstice she'd imagined, the longest day of the year just felt long.

The next morning, Martha slept in and then went for a swim. As she came up from the lake, Gray held out a cup of steaming coffee. She accepted it and went back down to the dock to drink it. He didn't follow her.

In the afternoon, she went for a walk. It was hot and the gold dog only came along with her for a few minutes before lying down in the shady ditch at the road's edge. When she got to the end of the lake road, she noticed the Fiat parked next to the small cabin and felt like she'd spotted an old friend. After all, their paths had crossed a bunch of times. She was standing there, hesitating next to a patch of cow parsnip Triffids, when the Fiat driver stepped out onto the porch. He was wearing green work pants and a white T-shirt. His hair was shoulder-length and he had a moustache.

He seemed unsurprised at her appearance. "You look thirsty," he said.

"Got any bubbly?" she heard herself ask.

He laughed. "No, but I'm sure I can come up with some kind of beverage. Want to come in?"

"No, it's perfect here," she said, slipping into an Adirondack chair on the porch.

After a minute, he came back out with two thick dimpled glasses and handed her a drink full of ice and cucumber slices.

"Cheers," he said.

She took a long swallow and tasted gin. "This is just what I needed." She drank and looked at the lake. "Are you here for the whole summer?"

"I'm here year-round." He told her he was a glass blower and he watched her shake the ice in the glass she was emptying.

I don't have to drink it, she thought when he placed another drink on the wide arm of her chair. "You made these glasses?" she asked, taking a sip. "They're nice. Shapely."

He looked at her. "These are from Mexico. I have some of my stuff in the barn, if you want to see." He gestured at a ramshackle wooden structure behind the cabin. He nodded but made no move to get up. He took another swallow of his drink and she did the same.

When he stood up and walked toward the barn, Martha followed, feeling dizzy as she stepped off the porch and the sun hit her face. She hesitated for only a second before she went into his workshop. She felt alcohol and curiosity buzzing inside her along with something darker. Who was this guy with the tiny car and the large mustache. She didn't even know his name. No one knows where you are, she reminded herself.

Then she was in blackness as the barn door swung shut behind her. Nothing was visible inside the dim shed after the blinding outside light. The air was earthy, dank and dusty. "You work in the dark?" she asked, joking but nervous.

"Here's one," his voice was close as his arm brushed hers. He placed something cool and smooth and glassy in her hands.

"Oh!" she yelped, scrambling not to drop it onto the concrete floor. His hands closed over hers for an instant before he moved away. Her heart pounded. He's locking me in, she thought. She wondered how long it would take Gray to think to look for her. She'd left the cottage without saying anything. Her hands were sweaty and the glass was slippery. A shaft of light came in as the man slid a side door open, and a table full of glassy objects lit up in the sun.

"Just what the world needs," he said coming back over to where she stood. "More vases."

"They're beautiful," she said as he took back the one he'd handed her and put it down. The curvy jugs were dark smoky colours, purplish green, brownish blue and they seemed to pick up the light from outside and hold it. They stood facing the glowing vessels and Martha let herself melt toward him a little, just enough to feel the edge of her shorts brush his pants. "It must be hot work. How do you sell them? You ship them out?"

Glass Man didn't answer. He put his hands on her shoulders, reached his fingers under the straps of her shirt and turned her toward him.

She felt the strange brush of his moustache on her mouth, then, the cushion of lip underneath it. She bumped the table beside her and glass clinked and clunked, rolling off, crashing against the floor. "They're breaking," she said. The sound of breaking glass frightened her. He didn't answer, he had one hand around her waist and slipped the other under her top but she pulled away, fabric ripping as she moved, blundering into the yard.

She scrambled down the driveway and twisted her ankle in a dip in the gravel. Her knees folded under her and she looked back to see him stepping out of the barn. She bounced back up before he reached her, holding out his hand, asking if she wanted a lift.

She walked away fast in the dusty heat, head pounding from the drinks, stomach uncertain. Halfway back, when he hadn't followed her with molten glass tongs in his hands or the Fiat in high gear, she slowed down.

Back at the cottage she fell onto the lumpy bed and slept until dark. When she got up, she downed three aspirin and a few glasses of water. Gray didn't ask where she'd gone. He put a movie on.

"I can't believe you want to watch this," she said.

"I like high seas adventure."

On the saggy plaid couch, they let *The Titanic* play. Martha was relieved to climb aboard. The story was clear-cut.

Lovers against villains. Of course the iceberg meant they never got beyond the first few days together. "Near, far, wherever you are. I believe that the heart does go on…" Céline warbled. Near, far, but dead, Martha thought. The beloved wasn't going to do anything aggravating that way. No years of winter or summer holidays, special occasions or all the days and days in between.

In the very dark country dark, Martha turned out the lights and they got into bed. Outside, a loon wailed, or hooted. Except for her throbbing headache she felt like she could have dreamed the murky afternoon.

"Where's your hand?" Gray asked, extending his arm under the sheet. For a second she held still and kept her hand clamped against her side. Then, after a minute, she reached out for his.

The Sweater

After school Magali was collecting stinking beer cans from the coffee table in front of the TV when the message popped up. "Going to C's place in the country. 🌿 🍃 🍄! Take care of each other, back soon! 🖤 🖤"

Mom had been all about Claude-Claude-Claude and lots of beer since she lost her job. At least beer cans had a deposit. Magali looked in the bag. A dozen cans, almost two-fifty. She opened the cupboard. Half a pack of spaghetti. A can of soup, a light box of cornflakes, mostly empty, a bit of margarine in a tub, some milk. A ten on the table under the salt shaker, probably all she had in her wallet the minute she got it in her head to leave town. Elsa came in and looked in the cupboard, then the fridge.

"She's with Claude," Magali told her, running hot water into the sink full of crusty plates and bowls.

Elsa watched for a minute, then dropped her head in a nod. "I'm doing my homework."

When the dishes were drying in the rack, Magali lay on the floor of their bedroom and wiggled pruney fingertips. She listened to the scritch-scratch of Elsa's pencil. Her sister did homework when anxious, which was often, but the small sound was comforting. They had ways of filling up the empty apartment. Hot water, soap suds, math problems and French homework. It was peaceful and quiet with just the two of them if you didn't count the stomach rumblings.

The next morning was sharp and bright and Magali shivered in her wind breaker. At the corner, she saw Béa and her boyfriend coming out of the Italian café on Parc, sipping foamy coffee drinks. Béa wore a sweater of soft cocoa-coloured wool, hair long and straight and shiny down her back, white shoes, jeans just the right length, perfect ankles poking out. The two of them talked and laughed. He tilted his head to listen as Béa spoke.

Béa lived two blocks over from the pharmacies, barren storefronts and rushing lanes of traffic on Parc Avenue, on a perfect quiet street with neat rectangles of front gardens and a mom, Catherine, who told everyone to call her Cat, and who used to help them make lemonade to sell at a little table on the sidewalk. The block was full of families with kids and they'd spent warm nights playing whooping running games of *cache-cache* hide-and-seek tag late into the dark. Now Béa's little sister played with Elsa but the big sisters had drifted apart. This morning, Magali couldn't take her eyes off Béa and that guy, Nic, who was always carrying a book and could be seen on benches in the park or on the street, reading. When it was sunny they took turns playing the piano outside the library, leaning against each other and singing. Now she followed them like a movie that had the sound down too low, straining to get close enough to hear what they were saying.

Everyone knew the old guy at the dépanneur didn't care about shoplifters. He watched Korean shows on the iPad and couldn't be bothered to look at the black and white tiles on the TV screen that showed who was on camera in the store's aisles or fridges. Magali absorbed a package of cheese into the sleeve of her jacket and slipped it into her bag. At the cash she paid for four bananas.

From outside, the little pizza place looked dark. At four-thirty on a Wednesday, it was empty. Magali waited until a skinny guy in a dirty apron came out from the kitchen. She slid the brick of mozzarella over to him. Without a word, he fished in his pocket and dropped loonies on the counter, just as she'd heard he would.

"Would it be possible to get a pizza instead?"

"Now you're talking." He swept the coins back into his palm, stuck a rubbery disc into a box, size small. Next time she'd bring him two bricks and get a large.

At their building she stepped on the slippery flyers scattered across the floor of the entrance as Ivan brushed by, mumbling "Hello, dear" on his way out, probably to the Parc Ave Y or the cafés on St-Viateur where he picked up butts from the sidewalk. He'd hold each one in yellowed claws and smoke it down to the filter. Sometimes someone noticed and gave him a full-length cigarette.

"Pizza!" Magali announced when she came through the door.

"Where'd you get it?" Elsa asked.

"Special offer up on Bernard." Magali felt her nodding sister deciding not to ask more questions.

Things would have been manageable if they'd just known what day Mom was coming back. When they called, she didn't pick up.

A couple years ago, back before the pandemic, on the Saturday of Magali's twelfth birthday, she'd been inside, putting up streamers and sticking balloons to the wall with masking tape while her mom spread frosting from a can on a chocolate cake that was still warm. The white frosting melted and streaked. Then Béa's mom, Cat, phoned from her cell. Everyone was out front, she said, where the building entrance was barricaded with yellow tape, and cop cars and emergency vehicles had their lights flashing. All Magali's friends and the friends' parents were clumped together on the sidewalk with bags of suits and towels for free swim at the Y and gifts for the party afterward.

Magali understood that her birthday was not going to be fine despite the balloons and streamers in the apartment and her stacking of flyers and removal of garbage to make the entrance welcoming and tidy.

"Cake at ours!" Cat had declared. She even texted people who hadn't arrived yet since she had their contacts on her phone.

Magali had lain awake nights worrying about the party, wanting it perfect, imagining winning enough in the 649 to buy a house next door to Béa's in time to have her birthday there. In the end the party happened at Béa's house. Cat served little cupcakes so cute they made their lumpy cake with streaky frosting look even sadder.

"Overdose. Fucking druggies," Louis the concierge had told Mom later. A bunch of guys had forced their way into Ivan's apartment and squatted there for weeks until one keeled over and the rest took off. They'd trashed the place and taken everything Ivan had. After that, Louis fixed the buzzer downstairs and at least for a while everyone actually had to buzz to get in.

"Bad cell reception here. Hope you guys are good! See you soon! I ♥ you."

Magali tossed her phone on the table with a clatter.

She tucked a piece of her little sister's dirty hair behind her ear and got a whiff of smelly kid and corny socks. "When's the last time you had a shower, Els?"

"Why?"

"It'll help you fall asleep. It's relaxing." Magali knew she couldn't let her sister go to school smelling bad.

On recycling night, they went out in the dark and collected cans and bottles from the street. At the dep, the woman who hated kids grumbled about having to give them money for cans they hadn't purchased at her store so Magali bought a Mars bar there and used a kitchen knife at home to cut it in two. After school the next day she stuffed two big front loaders at the laundromat next door, glancing at the warnings. How loaded was overloaded? She looked out at gray Parc Avenue as the clothes swished. Just in case people stole dripping wet laundry, she stayed put, waiting. Due to the Mars bar, her budget for drying was only five quarters. Everything was still wet. She hauled the heavy garbage bags home and she and Elsa draped garments onto chairs, doorknobs, and the towel rack in the bathroom. The heat in the building wasn't on yet so the next morning their leggings and shirts were still soggy and smelled mildewy. As she ran laps in gym the damp seams of her shorts chafed her thighs.

After school, Magali stood next to the Y in the rain, waiting for the light to change. With this weather their clothes would never dry. She looked up when someone nudged her. It was Nic, holding a large polka dotted umbrella, and motioning her to step closer to him and Béa as he lifted it higher to fit over all three of them. They scuttled down Parc Avenue as a trio.

"We're going to the library. Want to come?" he asked. "We're seeking spiritual and intellectual enlightenment."

Magali glanced at Béa, who smiled, a few drops of rain beading on the sleeve of her sweater. "Don't mind His Goofiness."

"I speak for myself since of course some of us are already enlightened," Nic added.

The library, in a former church, was just a few doors down. Magali and Elsa often went after school, especially if Mom was consuming beer and action movies with Claude. Under the umbrella Magali was considering the invitation when Béa said, "This is Magali's place."

"You live here?" Nic said. Most people walked by the plain brick apartment building without a glance. He looked up with interest. "Cool."

Picking up on his curiosity, Béa said, "We should come up!"

Magali squinted. There was nothing to eat. Their underwear was hanging from lamps. "I don't think so," she said.

"Aw, come on Mags, we just want to hang out," Nic implored.

"Another time!" She ducked out from under the umbrella and ran inside.

A few years ago, Magali had bugged and bugged and bugged her mom to get the type of macaroni they ate at Béa's house. It was Kraft Dinner but the natural kind from the health food store with noodles that were shaped like little bunnies. Magali found it on sale and Mom finally gave her money and she got three boxes. She made sure they had cookies, too, and carrots because at Béa's house they always ate carrots with everything. In the morning after Mom left for work she did the dishes and wiped off the table and the stove and even filled the pot with water so everything would be ready. Walking home at lunch, Béa scuffed her feet.

Magali said, "Come on, let's go. We have to make macaroni!" At the Hasidic fish store on the corner, they waited to cross.

"I don't know."

"You don't know what?"

"I don't know if I want to go to your place."

"You don't? How come?" Magali felt her lip begin to tingle.

"I just don't feel *comfortable*."

"What do you mean?"

"You know…"

"What?" Even if she already knew, she was going to make Béa say it.

Béa had faint freckles on her perfect nose. "It's creepy."

"My place?"

"Your building, those stairs, the halls, that guy…"

"What guy?" Magali couldn't stop asking for details, not that she needed them.

"That guy who had the thing happen in his apartment. My mom says it's not safe."

Magali pictured the boxes of macaroni in the cupboard. They only needed one, of course. She'd wanted several so she could take one out and leave the others on the shelf to show an abundance of macaroni, the good kind.

"Hey, I know, let's go to my house!" Béa said.

Magali loved lunch at Béa's where Cat made everything and then stood at the counter drinking coffee, asking questions about their morning. But this time she just shook her head and crossed the street alone. At home it took five minutes for the water to boil and eight minutes for the macaroni to cook. She sobbed for all thirteen. Mom was at work and Elsa was eating at school so she could eat as much good macaroni as she liked. She was so stuffed up from crying it might as well have been noodles and glue.

After school Magali passed kids outside the Boba shop, enjoying the melty ice creamy sweet drinks followed by the bouncy-chewy black bubbles of tapioca pearls that slipped up through the fat straw.

She considered shoplifting food from the dollar store, but it was risky. She'd seen kids from school get stopped by the security guard and told to wait for the police. She thought about jobs she might get. Sandwich Artist at Subway, cashier at a pharmacy, dishwasher. Everyone needed help these days, the signs were all over, but they all wanted people fifteen and up. Magali would have to lie about her age on top of her experience.

She looked for other opportunities. She discovered that if she went to the washroom during class the halls were quiet. Plenty of locks were busted or missing. She hunted for a debit card that she could use to tap and pay for whatever she wanted. She found lunch kits, textbooks, jackets with the odd loony in the pocket. No cards, no bills. Then, a tug unlatched the lock with the purple dial, the locker swung open and there it was. Hanging from a hook, Béa's sweater; a soft, inviting cocoon. There was no one around.

Back in class, Madame Labossière, the math teacher, snapped her fingers. "Magali? Magali? Are you still with us?"

She had her own calculations to make. *If cans are 20 cents and groceries are $100, how many cans do the girls need to collect?* She should just ditch class. What was the school going to do? Call her mother? LOL. Her stomach growled.

Someone was knocking at the door. Magali opened it a crack and saw that Cat had braved their building.

"Magali, is that you? It's been ages. You're so tall now! Is your mom home?"

"Not at the moment."

"OK…maybe I'll stop by later," she said from the dim hallway. "I just have a form for her to fill out so Elsa can attend the Fall Fun Day on Saturday."

Cat, of course, was a Girl Guide leader. Who even did Girl Guides anymore, Magali wondered, except people like Béa, and her little sister Julie, and Elsa, who had now come to see who was there.

"Oh, hey Cat! What are you doing here? Why don't you open the door?" she asked Magali.

"I have a form for the outing on Saturday. Julie said you wanted to come, right?"

"I'd love that but—"

"She'll bring it to school tomorrow." Magali reached out, grabbed the paper, and closed the door.

"What are you doing? Cat's so nice," Elsa said.

"Shhhh! She can't come in here, OK?" Magali whispered, picturing Cat coming in and asking questions about when exactly Mom had left and when she was due back. She yanked Elsa into the bedroom. "I can sign your paper for you, don't worry."

There was more knocking. "Still me!" called Cat. "I just wanted to say, there's no fee!"

Magali cracked the door again so she would stop yelling.

"For the outing," Cat added in a normal voice. "The girls did fund-raising for this, so disregard the part where it says $20. OK. I'm going to go now." She turned to leave then hesitated. "Oh, wait."

Here we go. Magali waited.

"Julie asked me to drop this off. She made this recipe to get her cooking badge and we have so much. She wanted Elsa to have some." She handed over a big container she'd pulled out of her bag and then set a loaf of banana bread on top of it.

For a second Magali wanted to open the door wide and hug her and pull her inside. Cat could come sit in the kitchen, or maybe stand at the counter and ask them about their week. If she did, Magali would tell her everything.

Heating up the pasta with ham and peas in a creamy cheese sauce made the kitchen smell good. The girls ate heaping servings.

"Did you tell Julie that mom was gone?"

"No, she just noticed I didn't have a big lunch."

"And what did you say?"

"Nothing. I said we had to go grocery shopping."

On the permission slip, Magali scrawled their mom's signature, thinking how dumb it was they always assumed only the parent could do that. She folded the paper and tucked it into the front pocket of Elsa's knapsack.

Saturday, after walking Elsa to Guides for the Fall Fun Day excursion, Magali came home. Alone in the apartment, she pulled it on and stood in front of the mirror. She would never be able wear it to school or around the neighbourhood. Maybe, if she could stand to let it go, she could sell it to one of the trendy thrift stores. For now, she just let it surround her. Dense and wooly, warm to the touch, Béa's sweater wrapped her in a soft embrace.

Green Eyes

Amber pushed the shovel into the soggy ground, laid the spruce seedling in the hole, and closed the gap by stepping on it with her boot. The first tree of the day poked up crooked, spindly. She stuck her shovel back in and shifted the soil around to straighten it. She wondered if it could survive and grow.

"Today I need a thousand trees from *you*." Lison had pointed at Amber that morning, cornering her between the dining tent and the van. Crew-members walked around them, pretending not to notice the boss yelling.

Now, out on the block, Amber set another tree into the slot she'd opened up in the soil. She smoothed the spidery root system so that it pointed down and did not bend in a J or a U-shape. Foreman Dan had showed them this, and how to line their planting bags with sphagnum to keep the trees moist.

"Hey Speedy!" Blake called from the next section. "Looking good. I like your style!" He brandished his shovel over his head in solidarity. Amber waved and stumbled. The clearcut stretched in all directions, pitted with puddles and weeds, dead branches and stumps.

At the end of the row her lower back twinged. She retied her rolled bandana over her ears to keep out the blackflies. Her ears were blood-crusted and swollen with bites. "Don't you think it's kind of pretentious to do something so unpretentious?" her friend Danielle had asked before she left the city. Amber heard chattering and looked for Blake, who was nowhere in sight. Then she saw the arrow of geese cutting across the sky toward what must be north, flapping and flapping and flapping.

Lison had given her clipboard of spreadsheets a thwack. "If you don't get your numbers up, you may want to reconsider your plans. Planting is not for everyone."

Amber didn't quit her job in the neighbourhood and buy all the gear just to turn around and leave after a week. Her father would shake his head and mutter about her manual labour caprice. Her shovel struck a rock and her arm shuddered up to her shoulder.

Cwonk-cwonk-cwonk. She felt for the geese: *"I just flew in from Florida and boy, are my arms tired!"* She'd spent the night planting in her sleep, even though part of her brain kept trying to reason, *"Stop planting! You're dreaming!"* In the cold early morning she woke with her shovel hand furled into what they called the claw, and she had to uncrimp her fingers with her other hand, one by one.

The Parc Avenue grocery store where she'd worked for two university summers would be busy by now, with lines of shoppers snaking up to her cash. She could see them if she closed her eyes, tell the day of the week by the regulars, the flyer specials, and the mood of the manager. If she didn't have to code in the fruits and vegetables for weighing, she could have done the whole job with her eyes closed. Scan, beep. At stores with auto checkout, machines were already doing her job. There had to be more to work than being a human robot.

She got the tree planting idea from a friend of a friend

who was selling his bags and shovel. She found a tent on Kijiji, picturing a sun-dappled clearing near a lake. She'd never been camping before. "Are you sure?" her mother inquired.

Foremandan ("just Dan is good," he said, but everyone used both words and ran them together) picked her up in the small empty town where the bus let her off four hours north of Montreal. Then they drove farther out, past any power lines to the camp in the mud at the end of a logging road.

At dinner she sat on the packed dirt, eating mounds of lasagna with Blake, and Cass, who was also on her crew. Blackflies bobbed around them.

"If we were cottagers, we would say, 'These flies are terrible!' We can't even step outside. Our vacation is ruined!'" Cass pointed out.

Blake put on a serene expression. "We *transcend*."

"As long as there's food," Cass agreed. "I could eat for three hours straight."

The first day in the van out to the block, Blake had asked Amber for her planting hand. Then he'd put thimbles of tape on her fingertips to protect them against cuts and scrapes.

"My mom showed me. She was a planter, back in the day."

"Really? So she gave you all her survival tips before you left?"

"Nope, not really." He put his tape away. "She died."

"What?" she touched his arm.

"Last month."

"Blake! I'm so sorry."

He pulled up his hoodie and turned his head to the

window. Together they watched in silence as the van rumbled past what was left after logging; craggy piles of branches and stumps. After that, Blake had stuck to her, as if bound by confession and duct tape.

"Did you hear the geese today?" Amber asked now, before she ate another forkful of pasta. "At first I thought it was you."

He answered with his mouth full. "Hallucinating out there?"

"I know what you mean. They sound like voices," Cass said. She was an outdoorsy biology student who'd been sleeping in tents her whole life. Under the spaghetti straps of her tank top, her shoulders were rounded with muscles from workouts on the university rowing team. She knew all about planting since her boyfriend, Alain, had done it for years. Now he worked as a checker, making sure the trees were planted the right depth and distance apart, and that no one was scamming the paper company by stashing stock, which meant shoveling hundreds of trees into one giant hole. Planters called checkers narcs. Blake said when he had to take a crap out on the block, he planted a tree on top of it for the checker to find.

Amber said, "I can hardly move I'm so tired. Planting in my sleep is killing me."

"You have to lucid dream!" Blake told her. "Envision a cool clear lake, jump in and swim. Then stretch out in a gently rocking hammock on the beach. I'll teach you."

"Ça va?" Jérôme, a lanky foreman with ropey arms, joined them on the ground with his plate. He was missing one canine incisor and the other was capped in gold.

"Great!" Blake replied.

"Ça va," Cass said.

"I like to check in with the green planters. You?" he asked Amber.

Jérôme probably already knew about her low numbers. "Still green, I guess."

He tilted his head and looked at her. "It's mental as much as it is physical. Sometimes it can be the people you least expect who end up really creaming it. I'll come give you a hand tomorrow."

"All of us?" Blake asked.

Jérôme winked and ducked back into the dining tent.

"Why do they call it bear root, anyway?" Amber wondered. "What do bears have to do with it?"

Cass snorted. "It's BARE root. Bare! As in, not container stock."

"Oh, right. What's container stock?"

"You are *so green*," Blake whispered, slinging a long arm around her. His breath was damp in her ear; she squirmed out of his grip.

"Try Icaridin," Jérôme advised her on his way back. "Keeps the pests away."

"Good idea."

"Very funny," said Blake.

In the van ride to the block the next morning Blake wrapped his fingers. "We think we've got a green job but we're all working for the man," he said, and tore off a piece of duct tape with his teeth. "Lison gets her contracts from the pulp and paper companies that pay her to reforest so they'll have more trees to pulp to make more asswipe."

"Wow. You should be a motivational speaker."

"Maybe I am," Blake grinned, passing her his silver roll

of tape. "Sure, maybe planting a trillion trees would help address climate change, but you have to let them grow for, what, fifty or a hundred years. The spruce we're planting? Lives about, I don't know, fifteen to twenty years before it becomes pulp for paper? How long, Foremandan?"

"What's that?" The crew boss steered the juddering van over the rutted dirt road.

"If you want to absorb CO_2, you have to plant the right kind of trees, in the right places. Not monoculture cash crops."

"So, what? We just leave it like this?" Amber flung out a hand at the logged wasteland punctuated by heaps of stumps and branches.

"Maybe let it reforest itself," Blake shrugged. "It'd take a while."

"He has a point," said Cass, who'd been riding with her eyes closed. "This isn't the most sustainable planting. But I can't think about that now. Look, when we run our own planting co-op, it'll be different."

Amber had hoped to trade the endless conveyer belt of plastic at the grocery store for something better. "What are you doing here, then, if it's so wrong?"

Blake cracked his knuckles. "Information gathering in my campaign against asswipe. Personally, I don't touch the stuff!"

"You're disgusting." Cass yawned.

Foremandan stopped the van and let off the first few planters, including Cass. Amber stayed in her seat, buying ten more minutes.

When the last planters got out, Foremandan told Amber he'd marked off a gully of brown water at the back of her section.

"Just plant from the road up to there and back. No point going in the swamp. I flagged the slash pile in front of it." A flutter of fluorescent pink tape on a heap of logging debris marked it off-limits.

By eleven o'clock Amber had a liquid pillow of a blister on her shovel hand and was hot and sore from bending. When a brown toad the size of her thumbnail popped out of the way of her shovel she stopped to watch it. Then she tracked the scurry of a spider with a round white egg sac on its rear end. Blake had a word for what she was doing: snail-fucking. Anything to postpone bending over again, even for a few seconds.

At the edge of the swamp, she looked at the brown water and wiped her sweaty face. She poked her boot in the sulfurous bog. Testing, testing. She looked around. No one on her crew was in sight. On the road behind her, there was no truck, no van, no tree-runner making deliveries with the four-wheeler. The coast was clear.

What would happen, if? How deep was it? Wondering, her shovel slipped, she wobbled, the heavy bags pulled her down. The bottom felt bottomless—silty soft—and she sank in up to her chest.

Amber shrieked as the mud sucked her down like the quicksand in old movies. Flailing, she got her bags off and paddle-splashed toward a stump to haul herself out. She grabbed her shovel from the edge where she'd dropped it and used it to hook her bags and pull them toward her. Gasping, she sat soaked, filthy, and stinking of swampy rotten eggs.

A van pulled up on the road. She watched Jérôme survey the block. When he saw her he got a shovel out of the back and strode toward her. He sniffed. "Hmm. Your *parfum*…?"

"I slipped."

"You didn't see the flagging tape?" Jérôme looked at the bright pink ribbons on the branches by the swamp then back at her.

"I was just taking a little break. I wondered how deep it was. I stuck my shovel in to see—"

"A swamp is a swamp. You're planting, it's flagged off. You can't plant in there, so you plant around it. You don't have time for breaks. Or wondering."

They looked at the bedraggled seedlings that had fallen out of her bags. They floated on the water in full view. Jérôme shook his head.

"Those are dropped bundles. That's a loss. I'll take care of it with Dan." He pointed to her sodden bags. "Give me those."

He turned them upside down to drain the water, buckled them on and went back to the road to bag up with fresh trees. Boots squelching, Amber followed as he stabbed the ground with his shovel, slipped a tree from the bag, bent to drop it in and stomped the hole closed. He was a gold-toothed pirate athlete, connecting one tree with the next in an unbroken strand of action.

"Boom, boom, boom! See? You've got to keep moving."

She walked after him to the end of the row, and turned back as he started a new one.

"Make sure you space out your rows. Keep them straight."

"I can barely see them. Once I've planted the trees just disappear." The ground was already greening up with new growth and the tiny spruce blended right in.

"You'll get your green eyes. Pretty soon they'll jump out at you." He kept going until they got back to the road. "Can you do that? It's not so much about speed but you've got to keep moving. Your brain has to tell your body it can do it." He handed her empty bags back. He'd just planted a couple hundred trees for her. "Show me."

"I need more trees."

"Go."

He turned his shovel tip up and propped it over his shoulder for a minute, resting until she came back. "It's about rhythm," he said.

"Rhythm," she repeated.

"Rhythm." The lines around his eyes creased. He was smiling. He reached out to knead her shoulder.

Her swamp-smelling body buzzed under his fingers.

"Doesn't matter you're not a bodybuilder."

"Don't you have enough people to manage on your crew?"

"You needed a pep talk."

She started a new row, following his, feeling his eyes on her. She forced herself to keep moving, tree after tree. She didn't check every one to make sure it was straight, or stop to wipe her sweaty forehead, or even swat the flies. She kept going, all the way until she got to the swamp. By the time she looked back, the van was gone, the empty road baking in the sun. He hadn't stuck around to monitor her rhythm after all.

Then she let herself stop, straighten up, and put her hand to her lower back. She looked at the long row ahead to go and the short one she'd just done behind her, and the hundreds of trees left in her bags. She plodded on.

Birds called, she stepped over a stump, broke ground with her shovel. Spiders ran with their knapsacks of eggs but Amber didn't stop to watch them or the cricket-sized toads. She dropped a tiny tree into the gap she made with her shovel and stomped it closed, reached in her bag as she stepped forward and did it again, and again and again.

The next day, on the van ride back to camp in the evening, Benoît was giving Marie a neck rub; Clara massaged Miguel's forearm, and Cass sat in front chatting with Foremandan about herons and grosbeaks. Blake grabbed Amber's hand and wormed his fingers through hers. His hands were hot and sticky like a child's, his fingers a bony tangle.

"Don't." She twisted her hand free.

"Re-laaax."

She reminded herself that she should be patient. He was grieving, after all.

That night she washed her dish, cup and cutlery in the hose from the lake and lingered at the campfire with the others. People were starting to feel familiar now, as if she'd known them much longer than ten days. Two weeks out here was like a year of knowing someone in the city. She lay in her tent listening to loons and for the first time felt awake after a day of planting. Rhythm. She kneaded her neck. Jérôme's shoulder rub reverberated.

In the morning she woke up in her tent and inhaled the blend of cedar, pine and spruce. At the oatmeal lineup, she and Cass noted new couples nuzzling. At first Amber hadn't understood how anyone had the energy. Now she was beginning to see how working outside and sleeping in a tent tested every muscle in the body and made all the senses come alive.

It was the following day when it happened. Amber was moving down a row in a light rain. One, two, three steps, shovel in, bend, tree in, stomp. Step, step, step, bend, place, stomp, repeat. Repeat. Repeat. She looked down.

There were no more trees in her bag.

She'd heard of this and never believed it actually happened. She'd been in the zone, planting without noticing, without being conscious of every single tree.

She did a thousand trees that day. From the road she looked back at her section. She'd done it. Even if *it* was planting toilet paper. A few days later, she did twelve-fifty. Fifteen hundred, eighteen hundred. She stopped showering. Everyone said the bugs liked shampoo and soap. Twenty-two hundred, then more and somehow she became less tired. She stopped falling asleep with her clothes on. With her new extra energy she thought about Jérôme's rhythm.

"You were right!" she called out to him after the vans got back to camp one evening. "I *did* get my green eyes."

He glanced at her.

"Aren't you impressed?" she asked. "I'm up to speed."

"It's not about impressing anyone." He went into the dry tent, leaving her to stare at his back.

Cass poked her. "Amber likes Jér-ôme…Amber likes Jér-ôme…"

"Shut up!"

"In case you haven't noticed: *he's missing teeth.*"

"He's got character."

"Ha! I knew it. He must be, like, *thirty-five*. Besides, better not mess with Lison's boyfriend."

"You're joking," Amber waved away a cloud of flies.

"Sure, he sleeps in the Winnebago with the boss."

The flies buzzed right back in her face.

That night she looped her arm through Blake's after dinner. "Hit me," she said. "Lucid dreaming. Show me everything you've got."

He looked at her, assessing this request. "Well, first, at least ten times a day close your mouth, plug your nose, and try to breathe.

Amber did it. "Mm-mm-mmm," she grunted through closed lips. "I can't breathe."

"Right. Because you're awake. If you ever can, you're dreaming. You're teaching your brain to be aware of when it's dreaming so that it can control the dreams."

"OK, what else? Show me, " Amber said, and stepped into the brush in the direction of her tent.

"Try pinching yourself. In your dreams you won't feel a thing."

"OK." Blake was probably doing the self-pinching as she unzipped her tent and pulled him in. She lay on her back on her sleeping bag and pinched her forearm. He sat cross-legged next to her and talked about meta-cognition like he'd never run out of things to say. She wanted him to know she understood his rage about the environment, and his sadness about his mom, but he kept rattling on until she reached over and pulled him down next to her. She'd had chicken for dinner; his breath said lentil loaf. Up close, his face blurred sunburnt pink, lips chapped. Finally, he stopped talking.

"How about another lucid dreaming seminar?" he asked as they washed their plates the next night.

"I don't think so. I need to crash," Amber said, regretting the need for company she'd felt the day before.

"You can't learn it all at once, you know. Takes practice."

"Maybe another time."

They crossed paths the following day, as they bagged up and guzzled water from their thermos jugs at the road. "Ever blazing hot," she said.

Blake loaded his bags and went back out without a word.

Amber ate an orange. She took off her bags and lay down on the dirt road, her head in the shadow cast by the tree buckets. She closed her eyes. Just for a minute. The sound of steps made her spring up into a sitting position. "Back already? That was fast."

"What are you doing? Spying on me?"

"Huh? I was having a little lie-down. Just a tiny one."

"I need a drink." Blake took a swig from his water jug and lifted more trees into his bags. Amber got up and went back out.

At the end of the fourth six-day week, Amber clambered out of the van, and eased into a sitting position on the ground next to Marie who was bottom-up in the plough posture, stretching her back. Benoît passed out cans of warm beer and talked about a triptych on planting he wanted to paint.

"What I'd give for a cold Coke with ice," Cass said.

"Ice." Amber held the word on her tongue. A cold glass, sweating with condensation, full of clinking cubes. She took a swallow of warm beer.

Paul was describing, scene by scene, a series about ex-cons on a ranch.

"Cheers!" Blake came out of Lison's trailer with his pay and knocked his can hard against hers. Beer foamed over the top and down the front of her shirt as he chugged his in one swallow. "You're next."

Amber stood up and plucked at her beer-damp shirt. After half a beer her tired legs were soft spaghetti.

Lison's desk was the trailer's dining nook. She was the only person whose white T-shirt stayed white. "I like your office," Amber said.

"Anything else you'd like to tell me?" Lison asked.

"You know all my secrets."

"You're funny," Lison said, without laughing. "Like what?"

"My numbers, isn't that what we're talking about? I got them up, and they're still up."

"Sure are." Lison studied her face, her wet T-shirt.

"So, what's the problem?"

"We've found caches of trees stashed in your sections."

"What? Which sections? Where?"

"You tell me."

"But I don't need to hide them. I plant them. I figured it out. Ask Cass, or Blake, or Foremandan. Ask Jérôme. He coached me."

"I will." Lison gave the space bar on her laptop a bang and went back to her screen.

Amber woke up in the dark to twigs popping. Rhythm, she'd dreamed. She sat up, ready.

"Amb, can I come in?"

She unzipped the door and scooted over toward her duffle bag of muddy socks.

"Thanks, friend." Cass unrolled her sleeping bag. "I was about to have too much fun with Foremandan."

"Are you serious? Isn't Alain coming up to meet you?"

"I'm in your tent, aren't I?" Cass curled up like a cat and went to sleep, leaving Amber alone with her questions. Just as she was floating back to sleep, footsteps crushed pine needles.

"Ammmm-ber!"

Her eyes opened. Still not the right voice.

"Yellow light! What does it mean? Do I speed up? Or slow down? What's your signal?"

"Blake, you're drunk," Amber said.

"I want to talk to you! Let's have some fun! Let's lucid dream!"

"I'm sleeping. Go to bed."

"Get out of here, Blake."

"Whoah! Is that *Cassandra* in there? OK, OK, then. I see the way it is. That explains it. Fine. Enjoy your night, *ladies*."

"Don't be an idiot. Just go away."

"Go be an idiot somewhere else," Cass suggested.

He stumbled away through the bush, calling back: "Amber, I'm sorry. Forgive me. I'm so sorry, Amber. Do you forgive me?"

"Shhh. Yes," she whispered although he was too far away to hear.

"Why does he sound like he's going to cry?" Cass asked.

"He's sad."

"You rejected him."

A loon made pip-pipping sounds. They heard Blake call back.

"Loon to loon," Cass said.

"Maybe I should go see if he's OK."

"He is definitely not OK, but that's not your problem. You barely know the guy. You're not responsible for him."

Fatigue glued Amber's body to her Thermarest. She fell back asleep so fast and hard she didn't even hear the screams.

"He takes a chair and sits with us at the fire," Miguel told them at breakfast. "We pass around the rum, right? We don't know how much he drinks before this. Then, *de repente*, boom! He falls—on his head—in the fire! We pull him out—his hair burning—," Miguel rubbed his scalp, ear, forehead. "All on fire. *Terrible*," he said in Spanish. *Terriblay*. "Lison drives him to the doctor in the village."

Chunks of dirt scattered as planters stuffed the washing machines at the town laundromat. If they'd managed to charge their phones, they wandered the empty parking lot of the town's only strip mall and took advantage of two bars of cell reception. Cass called Alain.

Amber texted her sister a photo. On the screen her face was brown, thin and covered with scabs from fly bites.

In the diner, their Cokes arrived but no ice.

"I hope he's OK." Cold bubbles danced on Amber's tongue.

"I didn't mean for him to follow my advice," Cass said.

"Lison thinks I stashed trees."

"Why? Wait. Did you?"

Amber shook her head.

"Then why does she think so? Is it because you're after her snaggle-toothed boyfriend?"

"They found them in the flagged-off slash in my sections."

"The lowest of the low!" Cass squinted out the window as if to try and see the tree stasher. "Alain says that as a checker he's found lots of stashing. Some companies even budget for it. They expect it. Most of the time they never figure out who's behind it."

The planters hauled clean work clothes out of the dryers and packed them into duffle bags and backpacks. When they finished, they saw him, leaning against the wall outside the laundromat, head swaddled in bandages.

"*Hombre!*" said Miguel.

"What the hell, man?" Paul touched Blake's shoulder.

Amber went up close to look him in the eye. "Are you all right?"

"Oh, you know, out of the frying pan..." his lips twitched upward then flattened.

"You look like a mummy," Cass observed.

"Yeah, what's your mummy going to say when you tell her you were so wasted you fell in the fire?" Benoît asked.

Amber cringed as a bus pulled into the parking lot.

"Here's my ride," Blake said. The bus door and its baggage compartment hissed open. Blake heaved his tent, backpack, shovel and bags into the bus's underbelly. He turned around and grabbed Amber by the arm. "Look, I can't really remember last night, but I'm sorry."

"Sure, wait. Give me your number. I'll keep in touch. See how you're doing," she said.

"*On y va*," said the driver.

"I have to go." Blake went up the steps of the bus and disappeared. Amber looked but the tinted windows made it impossible to see him.

The crew bosses drove back to camp, vans loaded with strangers turned into scruffy friends.

Lison came out of the trailer. The flimsy door clinked behind her as she motioned for Amber to come over. "Blake," she said. "It was Blake."

Amber put down her bag of laundry.

"He stashed trees on his sections and yours."

"But—what—he did?"

"I got the whole story when I called his parents from the clinic. I talked to his mom."

"His *mom*?" Amber stared.

"She told me Blake had been going through a hard time. They had a huge fight before he left for planting." His mother told Lison that Blake had demanded that she resign from her job as vice-president at Kruger, the company that makes Scott Paper towels, Scotties tissues and toilet paper. When she refused, he threatened to sabotage her and her company, and she kicked him out of the house.

She died. In her head, Amber heard Blake's voice.

"I'm not sure where you fit into all that," Lison said, looking at her with curiosity. "My God. You never know who's going to cause you the most trouble. I mean, I never know. Drives me crazy." Lison shook out her ponytail and twisted it up into a chignon that she stabbed with a pen. "You weren't so bad. All I had to do was suggest quitting." She gave a small grin Amber had never seen before. "Worked, didn't it?"

Amber gathered up her bulky duffle and lugged it through the woods to her tent. The ground seemed to shift underneath her every time she thought she understood. Her feet crushed soft pine needles. Blake had crashed around in the night, wailing to the loon. She'd been feeling guilty about having treated him unfairly and sending him on a bender. Now, she had a better idea of why he'd wanted to apologize.

She didn't tell Lison about her own lapse. That hot day, back at the swamp, when she'd been so exhausted and desperate. There was no point now. No reason to confess that—before she'd slipped into the muddy water, before the pep talk from Jérôme—she'd intended to stash a few hundred trees herself, and bury them, deep down in the swampy muck.

Picnic

Martha carried bags loaded with beach towels and sandwiches through the crowd of coffee drinkers who'd spilled out of the café and were now standing around on the corner. In the night, she'd been so hot she got up for a drink of water and as she stood naked by the sink, the fridge in the kitchen next-door opened, illuminating their neighbour Martin, pudgy in his underwear. She'd ducked away from the window but he'd looked up and waved. That made it hard to pretend she hadn't seen him, but she tried. You had to make your own privacy.

"Whee-eeet!" Noah rode up, tooting the whistle he kept on a cord around his neck. He wore a stretchy cycling outfit, and when he unclipped his shoes from the pedals, he click-clacked when he walked. "Gonna be a cooker," he said. "Where you kids off to?"

Gray emerged from under the hood and straightened up. "Come for a swim? I see you're already wearing your Speedo."

"Seriously? Yes! Count me in," said Noah, pushing off. "I'll be right back."

Martha said, "What? You didn't even–"

"Be nice," Gray advised, eyeing the dipstick, wiping it down and then replacing it with a click.

At their secret lake the smell of cedars floated on the air, water lapped at a fallen tree, sun warmed the towels spread out on a huge rock. When they went, they lay around in old pilly swimsuits, or nothing, and didn't worry about sucking in stomachs or making conversation. One time, after a dip in the lake, Gray said, "What's the opposite of déjà vu?"

"What do you mean?"

"I'm seeing this in the future, like a reflection repeated in a mirror," he said.

"Us on this rock, like old turtles?"

He nodded.

The AC didn't work and when they got out of the car, sweat glued Martha's shirt to her back. Noah crashed down through the ravine babbling. "Man oh man, this is gonna be great. Oh, YES. Am I glad I ran into you guys. Maybe there's a rope up there on that cliff to swing out over the water. What do you think?"

She scrambled over the fence past the Keep Out sign, feeling a new appreciation for private property and wishing she had some.

"I can't wait. I'm in. Oh-oh, what a spot. Sweet! Last one in's a…Mar-tha? What're you waiting for?" he peeled off his shirt and kicked away his shoes to rocket in with a big splash. "Oh. My. God."

Martha sat down on the flat sloping rock with the bags of towels and picnic items. She'd made bagel sandwiches and lemonade, packed plums, chocolate cookies and huge green grapes. She unfurled a blanket and got out her novel. Gray jumped in the water and he and Noah paddled and sloshed like dogs. She waited until they were way out before she slipped into the water and floated on her back. Cool and perfect, the lake rested against her ears, blocking out all sound. The sun was so bright she had to close her eyes. She flipped over and dove down to the cooler depths, opening her eyes to underwater topaz. When she got out, she wrapped herself up in a towel.

Noah jumped in again and hauled himself back out, shaking his head, flinging water onto the snowy hills on the cover of her book. "Did I ever tell you about my cross-country ski escapade up north? It was wild."

Gray looked out at the lake, ate a sandwich and then reached for the bag of cookies, giving her a goofy smile as if to say, "See, isn't this fun?" while Noah filled the lakeside with a stream of chatter.

"*Back country...telemarking...sublime...*" he was saying, kissing his fingers. Noah had a slew of adventures on file and employed a hostage-taking style of storytelling, forcing his listener to respond before he would go on and get it over with. "*My buddy...wham. He goes, 'my leg, I can't move!' Holy fuckamoly! You know what I'm saying?*"

"Huh," Martha said, complying. The burden of listening fell to her because Gray, enviably and infuriatingly, lay back on the rock and closed his eyes.

"*Sit tight...I'll ski for help...wind picks up, temperature drops like a mo-fo...*"

"Mm." She kept her murmurs abrupt to make it all go faster but that never helped.

"It was *ass* cold. By the time the park ranger and a medic arrived it was dark," he was saying. "I didn't know if we'd make it back to him before he got hypothermic."

"But you did." She reopened her book and glanced at Gray who appeared to be dozing. Martha tugged her swimsuit down and turned a page.

"Well, we had the skidoos! Turned out he'd broken his leg. Two bones, two breaks. Tibia and fibula. Brutal."

Noah lay down on his stomach on the rock and for a minute there was just the sound of a crow in the treetop and whirring dragonflies. "Speaking of fibulas...I ever tell you about that orthopedist I went out with? A brilliant scientist but she was just not interested in anything beyond bones." He shook his head. "And boners, I have to say. I will give her that."

A splash. Gray was back in the water. Noah dove in after him and they egged each other on to the other side of the lake. As their arms windmilled across the water the scuffs of their strokes got quieter. When they clambered onto the other shore they looked like small flesh-colored figurines.

Martha read. Gray and Noah swam back and sat dripping on the rock.

"One time, when I was seventeen, my friend's mom invited me on a secret picnic," Noah said, grabbing a handful of grapes. "I was so nervous."

Gray and Martha looked at him. Maybe it was this admission of nerves that got their attention. She said, "She asked you on a picnic *date*, just the two of you?"

"She did. And I had no clue what to do about it." Noah scrunched up his face at the memory.

He had the kind of hair that tended toward frizz and his round shoulders were going pink with sunburn. Studying him, Martha thought that maybe Noah had never gotten past those dorky teenaged years. The stories of conquest and triumph over adversity were his way of overcompensating. Pinpointing someone's insecurity always made her like them more, so she listened with actual curiosity.

"I almost didn't go, but I met her at the park. She was

pretty and had brought real wine glasses in a basket. I could hardly eat. I kept thinking I saw my friend behind the trees," he said. "I got out of there as soon as I could. What a waste. I definitely could not take advantage of the situation."

Gray snorted. "Those days are over, eh?" he laughed and inhaled a grape. He coughed.

"Times have changed," Noah admitted.

"Maybe not so much," Martha said, still contemplating Noah's inner adolescent when Gray coughed again and made a squawking sound. "You all right?"

He gasped and pointed at his throat.

"Water?" She put down her book and held out the water bottle.

He shook his head, got up. He tried to smile.

"You OK, buddy?" Noah asked.

Gray turned away, made a loud wheezing noise before he turned back again. "Can't," he rasped, pointing at his throat as he walked into the bushes.

Martha looked at Noah who stood up, his knees slightly bent, his expression alert. "He'll be all right," he told her. "You OK there, Gray? You just got to get that out of there. Need some help?"

Gray was making horky gasps. Martha didn't know what to do. Time thickened and slowed. "We have to do something," she said, uniting herself with Noah of the hands-on life-saving action adventure.

"Heimlich time?"

She clenched her fists. "Do it."

They went to where Gray stood hunched over a patch of ferns. "OK big guy, don't worry. I'm just gonna give you a hand."

Martha hovered, heart slamming. From behind, Noah wrapped his arms around Gray's damp torso. He fit one fist into his other hand and jerked up below his ribs, then jerked again.

Gray gave a retch and the grape flew out into the ferns. He slumped in Noah's arms.

"Better?" Noah asked, moving to one side so that he could see Gray's face as Martha put her arms around him from the other side.

Tears ran down his cheeks. He wiped his mouth, then his eyes with his hands. He cleared his throat. "Jesus."

Martha said, "I have to sit down."

"Thank you, Noah," Gray said.

"No more grapes for you," she told him. "Just applesauce, compote, custard, pudding."

"Those things should have a warning on 'em," Gray said.

"Noah," Martha said. "Heimlich Maestro."

They staggered back to the rock. Martha emptied the container of grapes into the bushes. A few rolled down the rock slab and made little plopping sounds as they hit the lake. They bobbed on the surface as they edged down the shore, floating on the water. Harmless baubles. You never knew what would spell the end.

In clingy damp swimsuits they lay down on towels. Martha shivered despite the warm air. Relief and failure coursed through her body. Gray lay next to her. What if it had been just the two of them alone, the way she'd wanted? She was going to have to get Noah to show her the exact manoeuvre. It crossed her mind that he hadn't been making up that rescue stuff. Noah, her hero, her new best friend. She raised her head to look over at him, tears in her eyes.

Noah winked and gave her a thumbs up sign. "You know, one time my brother just about choked," he said. "He was staying at my place and the phone rang in the middle of dinner. He answers for me and goes quiet for a minute and then coughs on his stir-fry and turns bright red. Finally, he croaks, 'It's for you,' and he passes me the phone. Turns out it's this girl I know with a thing for spicy phone calls. She thought it was me and got right into it. Meanwhile my brother, he's gasping for air with baby bok choy caught in his windpipe!" Noah smirked and clasped his hands behind his head.

"Shut *up*," Martha snorted. "In your dreams, a wild woman calling you up desperate to talk dirty."

"I swear to God. How do you think I got my Heimlich chops?"

"Shut up!" Martha repeated, laughing.

"OK." Noah was grinning at her as he stood up. "I'm going to see if there's a good branch up there on that cliff to hang a swinging rope from," he said. And he surveyed the rocks, trees, and water of the special secret swimming spot like he owned the place.

Parade

Fred and her mother sat on a bench in front of the café and ate their gelato. A woman with a fussy baby plopped down next to them and popped out a breast. Fred tried to look away but her eyes kept returning to the exposed flesh, pale and blue-veined. The baby clamped onto the nipple and was quiet.

Between licks of pistachio, Evelyn sipped from a tiny brown cup of espresso. "Just look at that little one."

Her mom was always telling her to look at something, which made Fred not want to look, even if she had been, up to that very moment, looking at the same thing.

"I remember when that was you."

Fred angled her body away from her mother's coffee breath. This squeezed her close to the breast-feeder whose baby was making smacking noises and little grunts.

Giovanna and Luigi, the café owners, walked by with their long-legged daughters. Her mother grinned and wiggled her fingers.

"Why are you waving?"

"I haven't seen them in ages. Those girls must be in university now, maybe beyond."

Giovanna smiled at them, her steps click-clacking in high heels. "Someone's growing up," she said with a wink.

Fred's mother said, "Tell me about it. I'm in for it now. We just went shopping."

Fred nudged her mother—hard—to prevent blabbing. She could not be trusted and was always saying whatever came into her head.

"It passes, trust me." Giovanna jerked her thumb toward her daughters. "I've been through it all a couple times."

As she walked away, Fred studied Giovanna, dressed up on a Saturday afternoon as if she were going somewhere special. She wore a caramel-coloured skinny skirt, high heels and a tight red top with a low V-neck. Her dark hair gleamed in glossy layers. Fred's mom wore shoes with Velcro straps and had a bunched up windbreaker tied around her waist. Her wiry salt and pepper hair curled around her ears.

"Her kids are older than me, but she looks way younger than you," Fred observed.

"She dyes her hair." Her mom shrugged, biting into her cone. "Let's go check out that art parade."

"No."

"What do you mean, no? Why not?"

"I mean, *no*. I told you—"

"You said you didn't want to be in it."

"I said I didn't want to dress like a bird or a flower or *participate*." The artists organizing the parade had delivered flyers asking residents of each street in the neighbourhood to come in costume to evoke a particular dimension: forest, sky, imaginary animals.

"We can still watch."

"I don't *want* to," Fred repeated.

Her mother's mouth flattened into a thin line. "You have no idea."

"Nope, I guess I don't," she said, without asking what it was that she had no idea about.

"People all over the place—Toronto, New York, Paris, Saskatoon, wherever, would love to come to an art parade in this neighbourhood. You don't know how lucky you are."

"You have ice cream on your nose," Fred said.

Her mother unwound the napkin from her cone. "You can't just stare at screens all day."

"Why not?"

"Hello, sweetheart." The old artist guy, who Fred recognized from the benches outside the café where he was always drawing, paused in front of Fred's mom and bowed.

"Gabriel!" Her mom smiled and for some reason touched her hair. She still had ice cream on her nose.

The artist wore a black cowboy hat with a flower in the brim, a wine-coloured velvet vest, and striped pants. He was pulling a red wagon and smelled of alcohol. Fred thought he looked like a homeless clown. "Coming to the parade?"

"We're on our way."

He tipped his hat and went in the direction of St-Laurent Boulevard. His wagon was loaded with a pile of what looked like cheese graters. His sculpture. The wagon wheels rumbled on the sidewalk.

Her mom nudged her. "Let's go."

Fred savoured the nutty-creamy cold Nutella gelato. "You should dye your hair. Like Giovanna. It would look better." She licked her ice cream, testing the flavour of this remark.

Her mother raised her eyebrows, which were bushy, wiped her lips, and finally her nose, with a little napkin. "I don't know about that."

"I do."

Her mom blinked. "Well, anyway. *I'm* going to the parade."

Fred popped the pointy end of her sugar cone into her mouth, crunched it down, and got up to drop the little napkin in the garbage. She felt thirsty and sticky. A flock of tourists on a neighbourhood walking tour squeezed around the people carrying yoga mats or pushing strollers. When Fred turned back to the bench her mother was gone, along with the woman, her baby, and her bare boob.

Earlier, before gelato, at the depressing Parc Avenue underwear store, the old lady had shouted when her mom had dragged her in. "SO TALL! ALL GROWN UP!"

Her mom loved this place. She called it an original *haberdashery*. The walls were padded with packs of tights and undies. A collection of bras pinned on faded cloth in the display window blocked daylight from penetrating.

"STARTER BRA?" the old woman inquired, coming out from behind the counter.

Fred studied the socks.

"We'll just look around!" her mom replied. "Some of this stuff has been here since before you were born," she whispered, spinning one of the racks of bras in the middle of the store and making it squawk. "But they have some new stock, too. Here, Fred. How about this? It's a sports bra."

"I don't like that." Fred pointed to the adjustable strap, the hard metal bump of it.

"That's to make it comfy."

"Or that." Her finger singled out a tiny bow in the middle.

"OK, how about this one? It looks like a T-shirt. A cropped undershirt."

It was plain, with a scoop neck and elastic around the bottom, no pattern, frills or bows.

"We'll each try, OK?"

"VERY NICE. NEW! SO POPULAR. BAMBOO!" The Underwear Shouter had snuck up on them and was holding open the velvet curtain of a changing room.

Fred ducked into the other changing room and bumped into a stepladder that was leaning against the wall where boxes teetered in a pile.

"PLEASE, TOGETHER. THIS ONE, OK!" The storekeeper shook the curtain of the tiny stall her mother had entered.

"I could wear this for yoga," her mom mused. "I may have to get one."

Fred didn't want anyone to notice the bump of a bra underneath her shirt or see a strap that crept into the neckline of her T-shirt. She didn't want anyone to notice anything. Every time she walked down the street another neighbour who'd known her for her whole life looked at her and said, "Wow! Almost as tall as your mom now, aren't you?!" Then her mother would say, "Yep, growing like a weed," and they'd shake their heads and talk about her as if she weren't there, which was annoying because she *was* there and didn't like being ignored even if she hated being noticed.

Now her mother said, "Remember years ago, when Lucie gave us matching leopard print hats and mitts for Christmas? You'd say, 'Can we be *matching* today?' Like it was the best thing ever."

Sometimes Fred couldn't tell if she had her own memory of a moment or if it was just something she'd heard her mother say a million times.

"I knew that wouldn't last, of course," her mom went on. "But if we had matching undergarments, no one would ever know." She removed her shirt and bra, elbowing Fred in the small space, and put on the plain soft stretchy bamboo one. "There. Ooh, soft and comfy! See?"

What was soft was her mother's belly. It puckered, like an over-ripe peach, or pizza dough rising in a bowl. Fred reached out to see if the dough would bounce back.

"Hey, no poking." Her mom peeled the bamboo bra off, over her head, and for a second her breasts stretched up.

Boob tube, Fred thought, which is how her mom referred to TV, or whatever screen she was watching. Not that you saw weird stretched-out boobs like that on TV.

"I'll step out so you can change." Her mother put her own bra and shirt back on.

Fred scowled at herself in the mirror and tugged off her T-shirt. Half-naked under the fluorescent lights, she shivered and pried the thing off its plastic hanger.

"How does it fit?"

"Tight."

"It's supposed to be snug. That's how it works." Her mom poked her head back in through the curtain.

"I don't need it to *work*. I won't wear it."

"Up to you. But it might feel good in gym when you're running around. Might feel better, even."

"I feel fine in gym."

"Let's get it just in case. That way if you change your mind and decide you want to wear it you can. You'll have it."

"Fine."

"What?"

"You say it's up to me, but it's not really up to me. You keep saying how I'd feel better, more comfortable. But I feel fine now. So, what's wrong with that? What's the problem with the way I look?"

"What?" Her mother's forehead rippled with lines. "No! There's no problem. That's not it. You're perfect, sweetie." She shook her head and reached around the curtain to touch her shoulder. Fred flinched.

"HOW IT FITS MY DEARS?" The shouting old lady reappeared, next to her mother, peering in. Why not open the door? Get all of Parc Avenue to come in to look at her. Fred turned away but the mirrors surrounded her, showing her hot red face, and her chest smushed flat in the sports bra. Her eyes burned.

"We'll take two." Her mom pulled the curtain closed.

As they were about to leave the store, Fred saw them through the glass door, crossing the busy intersection, coming right at her. "Wait." She grabbed her mother's elbow.

"What?"

"Just wait. Please, please, please." She tried to drag her back.

"Why are you acting strange?" Her mother shook her off and pushed open the door. "Let's go."

"I don't want to go out there—" she hissed, hovering at the threshold.

"Oh, come on, Fred!" Her mother was outside now, holding the door wide, yelling her name.

The whole gang looked at Fred, caught in the doorway of the underwear store. Lola and Lenore and Robin and Sabrina and Cleo and Juliette, all celebrating Juliette's birthday. Fred knew this although she hadn't been invited.

"Hi, Fred," Cleo said. Lola smiled at her.

Fred stepped out.

"Doing some shopping?" Sabrina inquired.

Their laughs twinkled as they moved on, each with her phone in hand.

"What was that all about?" her mom said, rubbing her arm. "Wasn't that Lola with those girls? Do you want to run along with them? They're probably going to the art parade."

"I don't think so." Fred stared after them.

"Want to do something fun? Go to the park?" Her mother started walking, then turned to look at her. "No? OK, no park. How about an ice cream?"

To express her resistance, not to ice cream but to everything else, Fred dragged her feet, staying ten steps behind until they got to the café.

Now her mother had disappeared. Fred went home across the street and down the block. The front door was locked. She rang the bell. No answer. She didn't have her key. No sign of either parent. She walked back, past the café and climbed the steps of the church in front of it, watching foot traffic flow in the direction of St-Laurent. People pushed bikes festooned with plastic flowers and ribbons woven into their spokes. A little kid dressed as a frog with wings ran ahead.

For a school project back in Grade 3, Fred had mapped

the neighbourhood: the park with its playground and splash pads, the rock-climbing gym, the Y pool and the library. She pencilled in colour the ice cream spots, pizzerias, the *croissant* and cupcake and bagel bakeries. She'd put in all her haunts on the blocks and corners where she'd spent her whole life. Sometimes she had a dream of flying over the neighbourhood, which looked completely different from the sky. She could see everything and everyone, but no one noticed her up there, which was a relief, because in the dream she was naked.

"Hey, Fred!" her friend Claire shouted.

"Bonjour Frédérique," called Mia, Claire's mom from the sidewalk.

"Come with us," Claire urged.

"We're late," Mia explained. "We were supposed to start at the park with everyone but we're just going to hop in when our group appears—so let's look out for the forest creatures." She and Claire waited for Fred to hurry down the steps. They wore shades of lime and khaki with cloth garlands of leaves draped around their necks.

"I'm not in costume."

Claire lassoed her with a garland. "Now you're in leaf! Come on!"

Fred let herself be pulled along. A barricade blocked St-Laurent Boulevard to cars. A police car crept along the empty street, followed by the leader of the parade: a guy in a top hat and wedding dress who made swooping figure eights on a skateboard.

Claire pointed to the pair of huge, knitted breasts strapped to his chest.

"Whoa." Fred watched five brides on roller skates come behind him, followed by a violinist on stilts and a troupe of people in red holding umbrellas streaming with metallic ribbons.

"I love their rain," Claire said.

Next came a crowd connected by one giant sweater with holes for many heads and arms, and other people carrying empty picture frames around their faces. When a fleet of walking trees and green people appeared, Claire and Mia said "Now!" and jumped off the curb into the flow of the parade.

Fred joined them and a tall man in a wolf mask gave her a green ribbon on a stick. She waved it at the artists and children in their colourful homemade costumes in the street, and at the spectators lining the sidewalk. Music from the marching band blared as she bounced along with Claire. Maybe next year she could dress up in an actual costume, something wild. She saw neighbours and noticed Lola and the gang on the sidewalk; Sabrina and Jasmine were looking at their phones. She waved her wand. Lola waved back. Fred was in the street. She was in the weird art parade.

On the sidewalk in the sun, she spotted her mother, standing, smiling and taking it all in. *Look at that. Look at them*, she'd be saying, if Fred were next to her.

Fred shouted. "Mom! Over here! Hey!" She kept waving until, finally, her mother's eyes found her.

The Word

Bap-bap-bap-bap, a tennis ball bounced against one thin wall of the bedroom, while hangers jangled in the closet behind the other. Sandwiched between the noise of his little brother and his mother, Alex wadded up a pillow and stretched his legs out on the bed. As he clicked to join the college English Zoom on his laptop, the bouncing stopped, the door opened, and Oscar leaned in.

"Get out of here! I'm in class."

"It's my room too, you know."

The door slammed just as Alex was admitted to the meeting. Like most people, he turned his camera off to keep his family out of the COVID Zoom. Witnessing Vincenzo's mother offer him a pastry and a glass of milk was bad enough. Alex had also seen one girl's roommate lift off her top and change into another without realizing her bare torso was on screen.

Now the teacher was talking. Something about the question of home.

Alex's mother came in, smoothing her hair into place. "Get milk when you pick up Oscar. There's money on the table."

He triple-checked, just to make sure. Video/audio muted. "Got it, Ma."

The teacher, shelves and stacks of books behind her, was talking. She expected them to pay attention and called out names at random to make sure they were listening, ready to turn the mic on and say something solid. Was she talking faster than usual?

The teacher played a video of a woman with a huge natural afro like his cousin Louisa. She was reading her poetry but there was no sound. Everyone jumped on the chat.

Can you hear anything?

No audio!!!

Are we supposed to hear this?

It pained him when the teachers had technical difficulties. It was awkward. Alex turned his mic on. "Ms. Wilson, you have to select 'share audio from video' first."

"Thanks, Alex. Let's try this again. I want everyone to hear the poet read her work."

This time they heard it. The sound drew Oscar back into the bedroom. "Who's *that*?"

"Poet."

They heard it all: the knife and the gun and the war. The violence and rape and insults.

"*Language!*" Oscar said, which was what their mom told them when they used a word she didn't like.

"Part of the poem."

"That's a poem? That's fucked up."

"*Language!*" Alex swatted him.

"What are you two giggling about?" their mother asked, peeking back in.

"Nothing."

"Oscar's swearing."

"Alex's *poem* is using bad language."

"Excuse me people, do you mind? I'm in class here. I have to find out what the deal is with the poetry. Any minute the teacher is going to ask us."

Oscar bounced out, thumped right back with Shreddies floating soggy in a bowl that contained, Alex knew, every last drop of milk in the house. "Will you *go away*? Where are my headphones, anyway?" Alex turned his attention back to the computer screen where Ms. Wilson was saying something about something.

His mother, back *again*, shoes on, purse over her shoulder: "I want you to clean up here. I can't stand coming home to a mess when you're home all day, can you hear me? So, the dishes, please, and remember to pick up the milk when you get Oscar—"

The teacher, white lady with gray hair in headphones (call me *Ms*. Wilson, she said, or *Evelyn*) was now reading the poem again, the worst part, the most intense—

"Wait, did she just say what I think she said?" his mother wanted to know.

"It's poetry."

"Poetry, huh? Some patient at the hospital yells that at me I don't call it poetry. That's what you're reading in English, eh? Focus on your science classes, my love."

After she'd managed to share the video, with sound, on Zoom—thank God for students like Alex who helped her navigate the preferences—and they'd all watched and heard the poet read her poem "Home," the chat popped with comments and Evelyn lost control of her college English class.

Why are we reading this?
Excuse me, but that is some ugly shit.
the HATE. hateful.
One word: RACIST.

"All right," she said to the class, a screen filled with names on black squares like some kind of memorial wall interspersed with one or two profile pictures of cartoon animals. "I see that the text has generated a strong response. We will get to these reactions, I promise. I can't monitor the chat while I'm talking so I encourage you to turn on your mic to join the discussion. Otherwise, please raise your hand with the button if you've put something in the chat, and that way I will be sure to see it."

"But, Miss, this *is* racist, don't you think?"

"What are you referring to, Jeremy? The whole poem?"

"The part in the middle."

"You have a point. We'll look at how the poem changes at that section, and why. I know you all want to jump right to it, but I think we'll gain a better understanding of the text and the poet's project, if we start at the beginning." She spoke to the bright light at the top of her screen as she'd been advised to do to simulate eye contact. She always invited students to turn their cameras on but, speaking of home, who really wanted to invite an entire class into theirs? As the teacher, she had to. Sometimes she taught a whole class and noticed only afterward that something revealingly domestic was visible behind her; the laundry rack, a brush fuzzy with hair, a rolled-up yoga mat.

Evelyn paused to click on the blinking chat balloon. One new comment, from Raymond, To: *Everyone* (but meant for her): *Convenient to ignore comments when you don't like them. Here's an idea: keep the chat window open so you can see it.*

Rattled, she swallowed and said, "I do miss entries in the chat, true. It's hard to juggle what I'm saying with comments people are voicing, and what you're typing in there. It is not my intention to ignore anyone." She barrelled ahead, explaining that Warsan Shire's process for creating this text had been to interview migrants, record the conversations, and distill them into poetry. "What is 'home' first compared to here?" Evelyn asked.

"The mouth of a shark," said Daniela.

"Yes. What else?"

"The barrel of a gun," offered Carlos.

"Right. And what do you notice is repeated in the first part of the poem, and why?"

"'No one leaves home unless home is…'" said Yvonne. "'No one, no one, no one…'"

"It's like the story we read last week," Carlos said. "It emphasizes how people have to leave home when staying is not an option. It's not safe."

Evelyn nodded. Class felt possible again. "The metaphors show that home has become unlivable, and so people have to seek asylum. As I indicated in the syllabus, some of the literature in the course deals with disturbing subject matter, including sexual violence and racism. There are several voices here. Those of the people who are fleeing their home in search of safety, and then—"

At that moment, her husband Marc wandered naked into the other half of her office, *aka* their bedroom. He was off camera, but barely, holding a towel. Frederique followed, whispering, *have you seen my hairbrush?* Goddamn it—Evelyn lost her train of thought. What was her point? Every instant of hesitation took her further from the poem and the students. She had to make her way back and get them to come with her.

"OK, sorry, where were we? I want to go over a few

key lines…" She looked down at her notes and papers wishing she were in a real classroom. When she'd taught the poem before, students got a lot out of it.

She often had to come at a text from all angles to get students to see how the words collided and reacted with each other. She'd assign a piece of writing, play a video of the author reading, ask questions, then read parts out loud herself to get them to notice as much as possible. Online, she repeated herself even more than usual because students' internet connections dropped in and out and if she had trouble focusing, what must it be like for them?

"As some of you were pointing out a few minutes ago," she began again, "when the asylum seekers are granted refugee status in a new country, another issue arises. Let's look at exactly where this occurs. And can someone tell me, who is the *speaker* here?"

"The narrator. The poet," said Daniela.

"Could anyone be more specific?" Evelyn asked.

Silence. No one wanted to be the one to say it.

"This is where it gets racist," repeated Jeremy whose profile picture was a dragon.

"As you've noticed, there is a shift here. It's as if the poet takes the mic from the asylum seeker and hands it over to someone else for a few lines," she said. Doubts sprinted through her mind. *Wait—maybe not a good idea on Zoom. Maybe—stop?* In the version she'd put in students' course manual, she had removed the last five letters of the six-letter word. Now she could skip over this line, censoring the words of the young Black poet. *It wasn't too late to change course!*— Or she could read out the troubling line, in context. Isn't that what close reading was all about? Evelyn glanced at the gallery view of black squares, the handful of avatars, and her own pale face. Wasn't the uncomfortable power of literature the whole point? She cleared her throat and read.

It felt like the day she'd slipped on ice at the top of the front stairs and watched her body tumble in slow motion, except on Zoom it was her tongue that went on without her, her ears filling with a rushing *waa-waa*, anxiety rising in her stomach as her voice kept going, her heart rocketing:

…go home blacks
refugees
dirty immigrants
asylum seekers
sucking our country dry
n—

She read from the poem, and read the word as it was printed, no hyphens, ellipses, blanks, or asterisks. She asked, again, "So who is the speaker in this section?"

In the silence, she answered her own question: "It is clearly *not* the Somali-British-now American poet who we just saw and heard on screen a few minutes ago; and this is *not* the voice of an asylum seeker leaving a dangerous place, or even a refugee in a new place."

The chat flashed again and again, a bouncing balloon at the bottom of her screen. She couldn't risk it; one click would fluster and derail her. Evelyn's hands were clammy. Underneath her desk she kicked off her slippers.

"As we were saying earlier, Warsan Shire's poem 'Home' expresses the idea that the migrants leave because home turns into a nightmare. It is no longer a safe place.

The poem also conveys the physical risk of leaving. The journey, the refugee camps—brutal. And the difficulty does not end when one arrives in a new country. This is the shift that we notice in lines 75-77—where the poet is parroting the hateful, as you've noticed, the *racist* remarks that people in the arrival country make. Shire goes on to—" Evelyn paused as the blue raised hand icon caught her eye. "Yes, Yvonne?"

"But isn't it biased?"

"What do you mean, *biased*?"

"The poem is racist."

"But is it really? Is the whole poem racist? I think if we look closely at those lines, we see that the poet is calling out racism."

Tamara spoke up: "I'm sorry but any story that uses the n-word is racist."

"It qualifies as hate speech, doesn't it?" said Carlos.

"I'm not saying that the n-word is not racist." Evelyn paused. She had to untangle herself from the double negatives. "I mentioned that the poet interviews migrants and chooses aspects of their stories to include in her poetry."

"She uses the word, though. And you did, too, Miss."

Slippers off, Evelyn's toes were now sweaty in her socks as she said, "I read the words in the poem so that we could examine the context in which Shire uses the n-word and see her specific purpose for doing so. To clarify, I was not, I am not, using the n-word *myself*."

"But Miss, you *said* the word—"

"This is a poem *about* racism, among other things. Does that make sense?" It was happening. The news stories flooded back to her. Students complaining on social media about teachers using the n-word in class. Evelyn and her colleagues emailed each other. *Don't we have to teach students how to make distinctions based on context?* they wondered. Isn't that our work? *Not if it means losing my job*, one friend said. *No thank you. Not worth it.*

Another raised hand. "Go ahead, Laura," Evelyn said.

Laura Johnston was one of the few who turned her camera on when speaking. There she was now, fair and blond, saying, "It's the people who don't like immigrants who are saying 'Go home blacks / refugees / dirty immigrants / asylum seekers / sucking our country dry / n——s with their hands out.'"

Evelyn scrambled to turn off Laura's mic, muting it too late by a fraction of a second.

Tamara turned her mic on. "You know, some people would really disagree with you on this poem. It is never OK to use the n-word if you're—"

Evelyn jumped in. "We're not using it; we're talking about how Shire is using it—"

"—not Black—"

"—deliberately—"

"—and now it's being thrown around in a way that makes me—"

"—to underline the problem."

"—uncomfortable."

There were barks of feedback as the video connection lagged and cut out. The chat flashed.

"OK, can you hear me? Am I frozen? Alex, I see your hand is up, I just want to say a couple things first before we go on."

Your internet connection is unstable, her screen announced.

"You all are raising many fine points," Evelyn said. Was

there still a class out there? If they were all in the same room, an actual *room*-room, she could gather everyone together for a moment. "I agree with your objections to this word. Shire is using it here to *channel the voice of a racist* who makes these comments. These lines shock and upset us by highlighting yet another kind of violence the migrants face. This is a *depiction* of racism, which does not make the text itself racist. It is a critique of racism. I'd like to end class today by stressing that we cannot just take a word, or a line, or a few lines out of context. We need to consider the text *as a whole*." Evelyn wondered if they'd gone to another tab to post the recording they'd made of her, the teacher, reading, edited with Laura repeating the same lines; terrible evidence to be watched over and over by anyone who clicked.

Alex's little brother burst back in as he always seemed to do just when something interesting was going on in class. Turns out his mother wasn't the only one to take offense at the poem. People were upset and of course Oscar wouldn't stop bugging him with dumb questions: "Does Mom think I'm going to be attacked by microbes on my way home from school? Did someone pick *you* up when you were in Grade 6? I'm not a baby. Don't you have better things to do?"

"OK, go away," Alex told him. "Just come back on your own, but be here by four, deal?"

"Deal." It was a quick, quiet deal, made seconds before Mom steered Oscar out the door.

Alex had his own questions about the poem but between his family members and the Zoom crashes due to the weak Wi-Fi, by the time he was ready the teacher was wrapping up.

They'd made it through the first scary six months of the pandemic. As if to compensate for the stress of working as a patient care aid, his mom worried more about everything else. She worried about Oscar getting home on his own and about Alex losing his motivation in his online college classes, slacking off, wasting the chance at university she hadn't had. Her worry made the house rules multiply. *Pick up your brother at school; set a good example; get good grades; no trouble; no slacking.*

He'd been staring at the minutes in the corner of his screen through his Humanities Zoom after the brain crunch of Calculus 2, but it was only when he ate a bowl of dust dry Shreddies that he remembered: get milk. Then he noticed the clock on the stove said 4:30. Where was Oscar?

He stepped into his shoes, all dinged up with scuffs—perfectly good, Mom insisted—and mask on, jogged down the hall past everybody's cooking, the smell of garlic and onions no mask could keep out. He zipped down four flights and into the September afternoon. So nice to be out! He was inside all the time. Alex felt better outside, calmer. He took off his mask and ran along the stretch of low-rise apartment blocks typical of Côtes-des-Neiges, each one with a sign on the front door about wearing a mask and keeping a safe distance in the hallway. He skirted slow old people and others dragging shopping carts. Where was that kid? He looped around the outdoor displays of the little groceries spilling mangoes and past the scent of patties from the curry house.

If Oscar was going to fall into something, it might be

the crowd of drug dealers at that had been hanging out at the park since he was Oscar's age. Even though she missed the mark on the source of the actual risk, Mom had a point with all her fretting. He jogged around until finally he spotted Oscar and the other littles with a soccer ball on the field.

***

Evelyn paced. After that class she looked out her front window and watched the lineup of coffee drinkers outside the café across the street. It bunched up when people got absorbed in their phones and forgot to social distance. She observed them, thinking OK/not OK.

One second, she was fine; a slightly scattered, sometimes rambling, but decent, college English teacher. OK. The next instant, she was looping over and over in a viral video, *"Go home..."* Not OK. Her pulse raced. She checked again to make sure. No urgent message from the dean. No journalist wanting her to comment on this video. Not yet.

Cigarette smoke drifted in the open window. She leaned out to see a young couple sitting on the steps, vaping as they drank their coffee. Café customers used their stairs as public seating and left bagel bits and coffee cups for her to throw away. During the pandemic summer, people had started setting up lawn chairs on the sidewalk in front. The Italian café had a reputation for its latte and its scene, which attracted people from all over the island.

In the kitchen, Marc measured spoonfuls of chia, psyllium husk powder, and ground flax seed into the blender. When she told him her students may have thought she was using a racist term herself he said, "Why would you do that? Why choose that text?"

Evelyn stomped to a stop. "It's a kick-ass piece of poetry."

"Millions of great poems out there."

"Not all so current, and so specifically about this particular tension surrounding leaving and arriving and home!" She flailed her arms, knocked a glass on the counter, making it wobble.

"You know what it's like right now. Why risk it? Why put yourself on the line like that?"

"I trust my students. I thought we could get at the bigger picture."

"I wouldn't. Not necessarily." He added yogurt and hit blend to mix everything up with a roar.

She texted Caroline:

—Situation!
—What?
—Taught poem with n-word.
—You can teach work that uses the word. YOU just can't use it.
—I said it.
—You said it?
—I read it.
—Read it or said it?
—Read it.
—Did you read "n-word" or n- - - - - ???
—I read what was in the poem: n- - - - - !!!
—😕 Any fall-out?
—Chaos.
—Hm.
—What?
—Be careful.
—Late for that!!
—Next time choose another poem?

Evelyn tossed her phone on the bed and flopped down to stare up at clouds speeding across the skylight.

With no restaurants or bars open and no gatherings allowed there was not much to do on a warm fall pandemic evening. To get out of the house and explore a little, Alex's cousin, Seb had started drinking coffee in different parts of the city. He'd check out reviews online and they'd go. This particular Italian coffee shop was good for people-watching. Comments referred to the long lineup at the take-out window as "the catwalk." Just a twenty-minute bus ride from their part of town it was another world. Parked Harleys, Audis, BMWs and modified Honda Civics were parked along the street in front of the café where people walked with baguettes or takeout trays of sushi.

He and Seb were sipping their take-out lattes on a bench when a girl carrying a giant black pizza box came along, chatting with her mom who said, "Really? I don't think so, that can't be right," in a voice that Alex recognized.

"Ms. Wilson?"

The woman stopped. Her eyes flew between him and Seb.

"It's Alex, from class."

"Alex. What are you up to?" She looked around as if she expected a crowd to appear from behind a parked car.

In reply he raised his cup. "You live around here? Is this your daughter?"

The teacher tilted her head and squinted at him without answering. In person she was short, something you couldn't tell on Zoom. She seemed jumpy.

"This is my cousin, Seb. He loves this café. Well, all cafés, really. Seb, this is my English teacher."

"You have some of the best coffee in the city right here," Seb informed her.

"Ah, I thought—oh, never mind."

"What? What did you think?" Alex asked.

"After that last class, I thought you might have come with the rest of the students for some kind of, I don't know, action or protest or something."

"Mm-hmm, the poem. That was intense."

She watched him, waiting.

"My mom didn't like it much," he added.

"Your *mom* heard all that?"

"Yeah, well. She works at the hospital and old folks have used that word on her."

The vertical lines between the teacher's eyebrows deepened. "My God, Alex. That class, what a disaster."

"Yeah. I mean, what I wanted to say—"

"Ohhh, you had your hand up, didn't you? I said we'd get to you, and I forgot." She slapped her hand to her head and left it there for a second.

"That's OK. I wanted to ask—I mean, while we're on the subject—I understand the poet is using the word to depict a specific attitude. I get that, it's just—" The caffeine was propelling him now, coursing through his body and speeding up his words. "Do you think it's worth people saying it in class? Because that one term pretty much blew up the whole thing."

She took a deep breath and let it out, nodding. "You're right about that. It was not a successful class discussion. Really not and that's—I'm sorry. My fault." She stood in the middle of the sidewalk, and people had to step around her to get where they were going. He noticed her daughter was staring at them like, *how much longer do I have to hold this pizza?*

"Anyway. We have to get going." He nudged Seb who was busy following their back and forth, ready to sit there all night to see what happened next.

"Alex. Will you give her my apologies, please? Your mother?"

"I will."

"Tell her I'm giving the whole thing more thought," she said, her nods turning to headshakes as he turned to go.

"What were you talking about his mother for?" Frederique asked as the boys walked away, all long legs, track pants and bright white shoes.

"She overheard our class the other day when we read a poem—when *I* read a poem out loud—and part of it used some insulting language to drive home its point."

"Oh, mom." Her daughter made a face and shrank her head down into her shoulders.

At that moment an image came to Evelyn of the way the 8 a.m. class must have looked and sounded to Alex's mother—the white lady teacher on-screen explaining just how not racist the poet's word choice was—as she walked by her son's computer on her way out to the hospital pulling on her jacket as she went, or maybe, after a long night shift—as she set down her keys, removed her shoes and arrived home.

Appetite

"Help!" A bark followed. Then the little voice piped up again from outside. *"Help!"*

Groggy in the August heat, Bern got up from his chair, went to the front door and saw something small and pink poking through the mail slot.

His knees hit the floor with a thud as he knelt to lift the metal flap that let in mail and kept out snow and rain. The pink bits disappeared, and the flap clicked shut. When he pushed aside the curtain on the door's window, he saw Connor running away, straight into her mother who was rushing to answer her cries.

"What have you done?" he asked, turning to Mabel, his heart slamming in his chest. She watched him, eyes shining, tail wagging.

Connor's little voice and the dog's bark had jolted him out of a doze. Now Bern examined the mail slot for blood, the floor for fingers.

Next door, he rang the bell. Yves appeared at the door and held up a finger: *One minute.*

Bern paced the front walk. "Connor all right?" he asked when the little girl's father stepped outside.

Leslie joined him, holding her daughter on her hip, legs dangling.

"Hey there. You OK?" Bern asked. Connor's tear-streaked face was solemn, her hand wrapped in a towel.

"Where *were* you?" Leslie wanted to know.

"I was inside. Where were *you* while your daughter was yelling at my door?"

As they talked over each other Yves lifted two palms as if to separate their words and push them back.

"You can't control your dog," Leslie said. "It's dangerous. I'm making a complaint to the city. It should be put down."

A couple months earlier, Bern had hit the button on the coffee maker and as it sputtered he let himself imagine someone was coming to drink it with him. He glanced down. The dog was chewing Triceratops-style, a frond of cardboard sticking out of her mouth.

"Mabel, no!" He tugged, then noticed the entire box of coffee filters was gone. He hadn't heard a thing. Bern touched his ears, trying to remember where he'd put his hearing aids.

Later, relaxing in his recliner, it came back to him. The previous afternoon, when a swarm of Ducati motorcycles had roared up the street to the Italian café, he'd yanked the devices out of his ears and laid them on the arm of the chair.

He checked the crevices, the floor, nothing. They were gone.

"It's not easy being a single parent," he told Sasha, the audiologist.

"Tell me about it." She touched his ear to adjust the new mechanism. They both wore masks and her voice was muffled.

"At my age, especially." His baby, Mabel, had eaten two hearing aids: five thousand dollars.

"Be careful," Sasha reminded him after she'd tested the levels and saved the settings. "When you take them off, file them up high where she can't get reach. Put them in the medicine cabinet."

At the beginning of the lockdown, Bern had spent weeks looking through ads online. The day he got around to taking the metro to the breeder in Laval, a young guy in a hoodie that said *Thrasher* in flaming letters led him to the basement where puppies tumbled on top of each other. Thrasher picked one up and set it down at Bern's feet.

"No schnauzers left. But she's the smallest. Runt of the litter."

The puppy sat on his foot, her little body warming his toes. He fingered the gloss of her floppy ear. She was brindled black and brown with a white chest. She licked his hand; her tail flipped and wriggled. "She's a terrier, isn't she?"

"Pit bull."

Bern paid cash and placed her in the quilted cloth sack he'd brought. On the way home with the dog in the bag he felt like he was getting away with something. Did pit bulls have to be registered? He tried to remember the outcome of all those news stories on the breed. She was six weeks old.

"Heel," he suggested. The pup trotted around his feet early in the morning when sunrise rinsed the sidewalks and garbage cans in a hopeful light.

"Good dog." He tripped. She wasn't in fact heeling but

trying to get picked up. She tangled in the leash and fell over. Then she bounced along until it occurred to her to sit down in the middle of the street. To avoid dragging her by the neck, Bern scooped her up. At home she nestled in the recliner, warm against his leg, her dark nose tucked under his elbow.

Before she died, Dorothy, semi-conscious, had flung off the bedcovers and thrust herself upright as if to walk away from it all—the bed, the hospice and morphine drip, the vigil he kept over her. Two days later, her hand went cold in his.

That was a year and a half ago. He ignored messages from the grief healing group connected to the hospice. He did his shopping and took out mysteries from the library, until the pandemic shut it down and made everyone almost as isolated as he was. His voice turned thin and squeaky from lack of use.

"Wouldn't it be nice to have a dog?" Dorothy had asked years before as they'd strolled around the block on a May evening that smelled of lilacs.

"Studies show that thirty per cent of the bacteria in urban watersheds can be traced to dog shit."

"I've never heard that."

"I'm a font of information."

"But now that you're retired it would get you out and talking to people."

"I talk to you."

She squeezed his hand. "I mean other people."

Bern watched Yoga with Adriene on YouTube these days. She had a friendly way of talking. He liked her long legs and lithe arms. Adriene winked and sparkled. He didn't bother with the poses. He just liked to listen and gaze at her, shapely and luminous with health.

"*Oui, ma belle, oui, oui!*" said a teenager from down the street when the pup sprawled on the sidewalk and chewed on her shoelace and that's how the name arrived.

"*Ma belle* Mabel," Bern repeated. "Mabel."

Bern and Mabel walked in the April sun while crocuses peeped out of the mud; the shady side of the street was still dotted with heaps of grainy snow. Kids clustered to see the puppy and Bern felt their attention spill onto him, sun after a long winter.

Four times a day he put a quarter scoop of puppy food in the bowl and stirred in warm water, just as the employee at *Croque en Bol* had advised. The dog took a few bites, paused, then gingerly stepped into the bowl.

Dorothy had been raised in a family with Labradors and she'd continued the tradition in her first marriage before she met Bern.

"What would we do with a dog around here anyway?" he'd asked her.

"Take it to the dog park, like everyone else."

"What if we wanted to go away?"

"You never want to go away," she said.

"I'm just not a dog person," Bern said.

"I don't know what I see in you." She put her warm arms around him. He smiled into her hair and breathed in her lavender shampoo.

He emailed Eden: "Got a pit bull puppy. When all this pandemic business is over you should come meet her."

Right away the phone rang. "Dad. What are you doing?"

"Walking in circles, looking for my glasses." He cleared his throat. He moved in an oval circuit, through the living room, into the hall, down to the kitchen, into the bedroom, the hall and back. Mabel followed.

"A *pit bull?*"

"I wanted company. You told me I needed a hobby."

"A pit bull is not a regular dog. A pit bull is the kind of dog you have to train. How are you going to do that now? Seriously, Dad. Why are you doing this?"

"You and Nina should come visit."

"Great idea. I'll be right there. Nina is three. The perfect age to meet a pit bull."

"The dog is perfectly sweet. Her name is Mabel. The kids on the block love her. They named her."

He noticed the puppy had something between her paws. After he hung up, he bent down low to see what it was. The arms of his glasses were missing and the plastic frames around the lenses were nicked with teeth marks.

"Obedience is important," the vet said. She patted Mabel's flank after her shots.

"I've always been more attracted to disobedience," Bern joked.

"She has to learn who's boss," the vet continued. Her mask had little dachshunds on it, but her tone was without humour. "Learn how to behave. Especially around children. Do you have neighbours with kids?"

"A couple." Bern's row house was in a stretch that contained children of all sizes.

He went to the community centre, where they all kept

two metres apart in the parking lot as Nathalie, the obedience trainer, told them how to get their dogs to sit, heel, stop, and stay.

"What's important is positive reinforcement," said Nathalie, who wore bright colours of spandex and looked ready to run.

"Good dog," muttered Bern.

"When they sit, you click so they understand you're rewarding them for sitting. Then you give them a treat. Soon they'll associate the clicker with a positive response."

Bern had forgotten the damn clicker at home. He looked down at Mabel who was busy lunging toward the other dogs. "Sit," he said. "*Sit*. Mabel, SIT!"

His loud command got everyone's attention, except Mabel's.

"*Whoa là!* Save the big voice for when they run into the street!" Nathalie strode over, pulling up her mask as she got close. "If you're always shouting, they ignore you."

"I'm a loud guy," Bern said.

"Mabel hears four times better than we do. Try whispering. Be quiet, quick and consistent."

"I'm not known for any of those qualities, but maybe you can train me."

Nathalie laughed. "Look, look, Mabel's sitting. Quick, click and reward! Quick-quick!"

Bern fumbled with the crinkly packet of treats. "Good, Mabel."

"Keep working on it!"

"Do I get a treat?" he winked but she'd moved onto the next dog owner.

On the walk/drag/tangle home, he tugged the leash. "We're bad students, Mabel."

According to Nathalie, Mabel shouldn't nap in his chair or sleep in his bed. She had to sleep in a crate, otherwise she might start thinking she was a person, or the alpha dog.

Bern got a crate and put a toy in it, as the books and websites recommended. He encouraged Mabel to spend time inside during the day, with the door open. He missed having her in his chair, but she weighed twenty pounds already. It was mid-summer and hot for cuddling. Also, he'd started panicking when he woke up and found her gone from his side. He'd lurch up from the recliner, stumbling to find where she was and what she'd eaten this time.

Connor wiggled her four-year-old pink fingers through the fence that divided her rectangle of front yard from Bern's.

Mabel licked Connor's fingers, then lost interest and bounded toward the gate as a border collie approached with its owner. Mabel gave a throaty rumble and a little woof. Better than barking. Bern looked around for the stupid clicker. And where were the treats?

The woman with the pug from down the block ambled by. Mabel groaned.

"Pretty good," Bern told her.

"Mabel, hey! Look at me! Here, Mabel! Here, girl!" Connor waggled her fingers.

"Don't tease her, Connor. Why don't you come over and say hi."

The girl pelted down her front walk, out the gate and over to Bern's. Mabel wriggled as Connor patted her head and back and rump and tried to get her to shake a paw. Bern watched from his chair.

"Connor?" Leslie called from her door. Her hair had the same coppery waves as her daughter, smoothed and swept up into a neat twist. "Come-here-right-now." Girl and dog both froze at the command, and one went straight home.

Mabel had no appetite at all one morning when Bern opened the crate. He couldn't find her leash, so he let her out into the backyard to do her business. In the crate he found a puddle of vomit. She was off her feed all day and barely moved.

"What do you think this is?" The vet traced a shape on her ultrasound screen. "I think it's the D-ring from her leash."

"I don't know when she ever had time to eat that," Bern said.

The vet looked at him, waiting.

"Maybe I dozed off the other night before crating her," he admitted. He looked at Mabel curled on the examining table. "What do we do?"

"She can't eliminate the metal. Your dog is in pain."

Dorothy always used to say, "Delicious! You're amazing."

"It's chèvre-betterave savory gâteau," he replied. "Lemon-zaatar fattoush with roasted brussel sprouts; green beans with mustard seeds; pomegranate tofu and spicy sumac eggplant."

"If it weren't for you, I'd be eating peanut butter sandwiches."

"You wouldn't even mind."

"But I like this better. Remember that cardamom coffee? It was cold and we'd been walking around for hours and when we got home you made a fresh pot of espresso at four in the afternoon? That was the best cup of coffee of my life. And the biscotti…" It wasn't just food. Dorothy could soak up the flavour of a moment and relive it with intensity; she had a talent for happiness, for seeing the good side.

When he asked the dog park people if they'd read any good books lately what he really wanted was for them to ask *him* what he'd been reading and what *he* thought. Dorothy's curiosity had always made him craft a clever assessment. He missed her delight in him, her appetite for whatever he concocted.

When she got sick, Bern's cooking, even his soups, Tuscan white bean, chicken noodle, pumpkin velouté, had gone uneaten. Family and friends swooped in to take her to appointments and ask questions first of one specialist and then another and eventually the hospice nurses and chaplains and social workers. Everyone was more helpful than he was. Bern sat close by and turned pages even though his fear was so distracting he couldn't follow any plot.

After surgery ($1500) to remove the metal part of the leash, Bern ditched errands midway and raced back in a panic. Had he crated her? His grocery shopping turned sparse and spotty: ham, berries, a jar of artichoke hearts. When he got home, he found Mabel quiet in her crate, dark eyes shining, head cocked. "What am I going to do with you?" he asked letting her out to whap her tail against his legs in welcome.

THE TALLY
- one pair of glasses
- two hearing aids (the expensive kind)
- one leash (nylon strap plus hardware)
- a rag rug (thrown into the crate before noticing the next day that her poop was rag-like)
- a box of coffee filters (full)
- shoes (many)
- rubber bands (uncountable)

And now Mabel had ingested the hard plastic lining of her crate. It was August. The dog turned in circles in search of a comfortable position.

The vet kept her overnight.

Bern ordered the Cadillac of wire crates with a coated metal bottom, overnight delivery. In bed, he tossed to dreams of Mabel circling in distress.

She was released after scans and observation ($500).

"Our lucky day, girl! No surgery!" He put his arms around her, patting her side. When he stopped, she poked her blunt nose under his hand for more. Bern fastened the new chew-proof leash to her collar.

At home, they celebrated. Bern stood at the sink and spooned strawberry jam out of the jar while Mabel crunched her kibble. He didn't bother cooking anymore. The blobs of jellied fruit slid around his mouth. When a spoonful spilled, Mabel helped clean up. The floor was sticky. He didn't care. Bern deleted another message from the grief group.

After Leslie said Mabel was dangerous and should be put down, Yves made more of his *break-it-up, break-it-up* gestures.

"But I always mail Mabel cookies through the door!" Connor said.

"What did you say?" Leslie set her daughter down with a thump. "You've done this before?"

"Animal crackers are her favourite. I always take my hand out after Mabel eats the cookies. But this time—"

"Mabel bit you," her mother prompted. "You said it hurt."

"Mabel was licking my fingers and it tickled so much I twisted. I got stuck—" Connor held up her hand. A thin scrape marked her wrist. "She ate the bears and lions and elephants and everything. The door bit me."

Leslie exhaled, shaking her head.

If there had been a bite, they wouldn't have been standing around talking. Bern knew that, but the pale star of Connor's fingers spread wide, unbloodied and whole, filled him with relief.

Even so, there was always going to be something. It could have been worse. But he lost his nerve.

On a warm September Saturday, Nathalie rang his doorbell wearing rainbow leggings, fluorescent green trainers, and a raspberry mask. *"Bonjour!* Your taxi's here!"

Bern loaded the deluxe super crate into her station wagon and opened the crate door. Mabel hopped in. As Nathalie drove over the bridge to the south shore the sun sparkled on the pleats in the river. "Thank you for this," he said.

"MJ really *gets* high energy dogs and she has a great place," Nathalie said. "This makes sense."

His breath was hot inside the mask. He noticed a splotch of coffee on the shirt stretched tight over his belly and tugged his jacket closed. "I thought it made sense for me to have a dog."

"Mabel is just too *much* dog, Bernard."

"Well, I'm not much of anything."

"She'd be too much for most people."

They got off the highway and turned onto a smaller road that curved past grassy fields. At a low house with a wide lawn in front and more behind, they turned in. A silver-haired woman waited on the driveway. She and Nathalie bumped elbows.

"You can't stay," Marie Josée informed him. "Pass me the leash and I'll get Mabel. Then you can give me her things, and Nathalie will take you home."

Bern looked down at the leash in his hand and passed it to her. When Mabel bounded out of the car, MJ grabbed her collar and commanded, *"Assieds-toi."* The dog sat. MJ clicked her clicker, gave Mabel a treat from a pouch strapped around her waist, and clipped on the leash. "Good girl."

"Welcome to your new life," Bern murmured. "Bye Mabel."

Hearing her name, Mabel wagged her tail. "It's better this way," MJ announced.

Nathalie backed down the drive. "She's right, you know. If we stuck around Mabel would just be confused. You'll visit someday."

"Take me back to my crate," Bern said.

"What are you doing now?" Connor's voice came through the spirea bush in the corner of the yard.

"Want to help me look for snails?"

"I have to ask." Connor slammed inside and back out, down her front walk and up his, to crouch by Bern's marigolds still hanging on even in October.

"You're allowed?"

"If I don't get close."

"Can't be too careful," Bern agreed. The pandemic wasn't over yet. He and Leslie were back on speaking terms after the animal crackers through the mail slot, but barely.

"Do you miss Mabel?"

He thought about this. Earlier, at the grocery store, he'd shopped calmly with a list: flour, pasta, rice, olive oil. When he got home, he'd lingered in his chair outside; no need to rush in, mask dangling; there were no surprises waiting. There was nothing waiting for him at all.

"Mabel was always happy to see me," he told Connor. He missed how she'd greeted him in the morning, or even after he'd disappeared into the shower for five minutes.

These days he walked in slow circles in search of the glasses and hearing aids he'd put down. Things were where he left them, even if they took time to reveal themselves.

"I miss her," Connor said.

Bern squinted. He took off his glasses and rubbed his eyes. He'd been an idiot. He saw that now. He should have got a dog back when Dorothy wanted one. He felt the layered ache of missed opportunity, on top of the other grief. Dorothy would have shown him how to do it right. Now he missed her more, and Mabel, too. Part of him still expected Mabel's nails to click down the hall into the living room, the same way, even two years later, he still waited for Dorothy to come get in bed at night after she finished in the bathroom.

"There's one," he said to Connor and pointed out the yellow garden snail. It was the kind that never seemed to be moving at all but shifted places when you weren't looking.

— for my father

Catch

JORDAN groaned.

Her mother poked her, again. "Could you please? It's 12:30. You have to do something today, OK? When's the last time you had a shower?"

"Who. Cares." Jordan blinked at the dull hot light blaring through the window. "What's the point. Everything is boring."

"Boring is good," her mother patted her leg. "If we're bored it means we're healthy and that's what counts right now."

"Old people are already boring so they like it. Quarantine is perfect for you."

Her mother opened her mouth to reply, then exhaled and left the room.

Jordan stuffed her hair into a ponytail, pulled on a pair of cut-offs and jammed a mask in her pocket. She went out to meet Fred at their park bench. "What is there to look forward to?" she wanted to know.

"Nothing," Frederique admitted.

"This vaccine, it's how many years away?"

Fred shrugged. "A couple? No one knows. Why's that guy staring at us?"

"What guy?"

"Over there, in the car." Fred pointed to a gray parked car that had a bumper patched up with duct tape.

"Who knows." Jordan squinted. The driver, unsmiling, seemed to nod at her.

Summer 2020. They were tired of all the neighbourhood's gourmet treats: the plastic cups of iced latte; the cold cones of artisanal ice cream; the pizza slices with fresh basil and bocconcini.

Jordan wanted something new. Or maybe something old. She wanted to goof around on the bus and go to a movie *in a cinema*. She wanted to share a giant order of poutine with friends without worrying about handwashing or aerosol droplets.

She and Fred walked, trading their parents' reasons for not getting them phones. "So important to do something that's not on a screen," Fred recited.

"Makes you more creative. And a better reader."

"Good for your concentration."

They passed a couple texting as they walked side by side. "This is a phone-free zone," Jordan informed them. They didn't notice.

At the splash pad they stepped into the fog of cold mist with the little kids. When Fred had to leave for a Zoom with her grandma, Jordan dried off in the sun and trudged back toward her place alone. She tried walking the familiar blocks with her eyes closed, which turned the street into a dark, dizzying terrain. She opened her eyes to find a mom shrinking away from her with a two-year-old in her arms.

"Oh, sorry." Jordan closed her eyes again and continued the solo game of blind man's bluff.

"Hold it right there. Don't move. Police," said a voice out of nowhere. Someone grabbed Jordan's arm, pulling hard. "We've got some questions for you." He yanked her to a car, slapped on—*handcuffs?*—pushed her into the backseat. "We know you've been dealing. You're coming with me."

"What's going on?" Jordan asked. "Dealing what?"

"Quiet!" he barked.

The car door slammed and she was stuck. How had this happened, in a car with a stranger? "I didn't do anything, let me go!"

"Shut up." The guy got behind the wheel.

As the car moved, she turned to see the sidewalk mom put her toddler down and reach for her phone. The man was that guy in the car from the park, she realized, the one who'd been watching them. "Help!" she yelled through closed windows. *"Help me!"*

The driver reached back for her, trying to pull a headband down to cover her eyes. Jordan flung herself away from him, shaking her head and twisting so her back was against the door. "Shut up, you little cunt!" he drove with one arm, swatting at her with the other.

Looking out the window she saw the baristas on break outside the café and the artist who was always on the corner drawing in his notebook. She yelled and kicked at the driver's reaching arm, glad she'd been doing quarantine workouts on YouTube, her cuffed hands behind her back, searching for the door handle, what if he'd locked it, he kept shouting *shutthefuckup*, she pulled the latch, the door opened—her elbow, knees, ankle scraping the ground—

GABRIEL squinted. Caught sight of a yelling girl, bare legs, bloody knees, a car tearing off. His pen scratched the page of his sketch book. People by the café raised their phones to get a picture of the receding vehicle, back door swinging wide. Then he saw someone—was that an actual nun?—hold out a hand to the girl who'd tumbled from the moving car.

Something was always happening, you just had to be there to catch it. Gabriel's motto: catch and sketch. People were hungry to know how he took what was right in front of them and made something out of it. To find out, they supplied him with falafel, pizza, paper cups of espresso, beer, wine in exchange for a peek at his sketchbook.

He drew the long legs, the girl's hair blooming in disarray, the car leaving.

The cops pulled up, lights flashing. The other day, he'd opened his eyes to police boots, wicked crick in his neck, cheek against the pavement and a cop bellowing, "Up, up, come on. Let's go!" Gabriel had pushed himself upright and assumed his usual position with his sketchpad. The city had set up the tables to give people someplace to go during the pandemic and this one had become his studio. He must have slipped off the bench at some point in the night. With a crowd of observant coffee drinkers lined up outside the café, the cop had left him alone.

Now he dropped his pencil case into his plastic bag next to a bottle, still sloshing, not empty yet. His sketchbook was full. Later he'd catch Irene and talk her into getting him a new one. She'd already gone straight to the girl and the nun and was making it her business to sort it all out. He knew she had her own bad habit; an addiction to lost and wayward cases. He stood up, ripped out the last page and before he ambled off down the alley, he gave it to—

IRENE, who, busy talking to a cop, only looked down a few minutes later to find one of Gabriel's drawings in her hand. Had he passed it to her while she'd been talking? She looked around. He was nowhere to be found. Irene strode back over to the cop car, waving the paper.

"Seriously?" the cop said. "I've got pictures people took with their phones and you're giving me a drawing?"

"It might save you from going through a lot of blurry photos," Irene replied. Gabriel was a mess these days, but she trusted his eye. Despite the look and smell of him, he still had the ability to get someone down on paper in a few lines. That's why the girl from the rotisserie gave him chicken sandwiches and the café guys brought him free coffee. His sketch outlined the back of a car, side door open, a blur of limbs, and there, clearly noted, the license plate.

"You think the number's good?"

"Try it."

The cop touched his collarbone and talked into the radio.

Irene recognized the girl from down the street. She used to see her drinking *babyccino* foamy milk at the café with her parents who ran the health food store. They had arrived and sat with her now, the mother on one side, the father on the other.

The girl would need something after this, Irene thought. Some kind of buffer. That nun. She had to talk to her. She looked around and saw the woman in the brown habit, the black veil walking away in her Birkenstocks. The words formed as she caught up and reached out—

LOUISE felt a tap on her shoulder and turned.

"Wait. You're from over there, the Carmelites?" The woman who'd stopped her gestured in the opposite direction of Parc Avenue.

Louise nodded.

"How would you feel about a guest?" the woman asked.

Louise experienced a jolt. The day before, she had swallowed her filling along with half a molar and a bite of carrot. Now when she chewed or grazed her tongue against what was left of her tooth, it zinged.

During free time, when they took a break from their vows of silence, Marie had said, "You really want to risk going to the dentist? An enclosed space with other people?"

Louise had tilted her head and slid her eyes sideways to encompass everyone in their enclosed space.

"Oh, come on, that's different. We're not going to infect each other," Marie said.

"Don't you think we may be infected with something other than COVID?"

"What are you talking about, Louise?"

The Carmelite convent had been built for twenty-one sisters a century ago. Now there were just twelve of them, experts at sheltering in place. In the spring when the pandemic was brand new, Louise had gone to Anne-Laure, the elected prioress. "It took each of us years to get used to this. How do you think everyone out there is adjusting?"

Anne-Laure said, "What do you propose we do? Hold a conference?"

"We could post tips for coping with confinement." People thought it was strange that cloistered nuns used the internet, but they had a simple website where they posted the necessary announcements.

"That's an idea."

"What if we opened the garden to the public?" Louise asked. They had their own walled park with a row of cedars along the edge and leafy paths under the lindens, the hazelnut, and other fruit trees.

"If we opened the garden," Anne-Laure paused, "people would swarm in like bees."

"Because they're all stuck at home in small apartments. They're living like us, with less space, less preparation, and a lot less prayer. Doesn't it seem selfish to have all this to ourselves?"

"How would we manage it?"

"We could keep the inner courtyard just for us," Louise suggested. This was a stone plaza with a statue of Saint Teresa and a few bushes. They all knew, from the news stories Anne-Laure read aloud during free time that every public green space in the city was overflowing with people and garbage. The sirens had pierced Louise's contemplation. The ongoing unease of the city was unsettling.

They had a vote by secret ballot.

The garden stayed closed.

Walking out beyond the walls toward her emergency dental appointment, Louise had heard shouting. There was a girl in the street, screaming, knees bleeding. Louise had helped her to a picnic table. This woman had joined them, for which she was grateful. She called the authorities on her cell phone. She asked the girl for her mother's number and called that. Louise and the girl sat together watching the sturdy blond woman, Irene, in action. She met the police and shepherded them over. A homeless man handed her a paper which she accepted without a glance. When the girl's parents arrived, Louise stood up and edged away to make room. The girl didn't notice her leaving. Was there still time to get to her appointment? She didn't wear a watch. How long had she been here?

She was walking to the dentist when that woman came after her, asking if they could make an exception.

JORDAN gasped. A rope held her down. Blindfolded, her heart slammed in the dark.

A bell was chiming.

Awareness sifted through bad dreams. She pulled on her robe, wrapping herself in relief, stepping into her sandals.

A light knock on the door.

Louise stood waiting. Together, they moved down the hall, joining the others. They took their seats along the wall. Facing each other, the women sang.

Jordan had never gone to church. The voices washed over her as her mind wandered. Soft morning light came through the window.

When it came back to her—the man, the grabbing-cuffing-shoving her into the car—she pushed it away. Avoiding it here was possible. Going back to the street she'd walked down thousands of times would be harder.

They ate without speaking on small tables for one arranged along both sides of a narrow room. Inside the tall walls, it was as if she'd fled the city and the quarantine. The bells rang to signal it was time for prayer, which was often. Practically constant.

She imagined trying to describe her cloistered week, and Fred saying, "It sounds creepy, very *Handmaid's Tale*."

"But I was free to leave anytime," Jordan would counter. That bossy woman from down the street had proposed it. Irene. She'd said it would be a getaway nearby, someplace completely different, right here.

The schedule reminded Jordan of summers at sleepaway camp where she'd had something specific to do every hour of the day.

She grated bags of carrots and sliced cucumbers for salad and ironed white cloths in the laundry. Louise, wordlessly, showed her how to pour batter between the massive iron plates of a smooth waffle iron to make host. Afterward, they punched out the thin round wafers and packed them into bags for the diocese. The extra in-between pieces, the unholy bits, were picked up by a distributor who sold bags of the crunchy cuttings to grocery stores and *dépanneurs* as snacks.

What was excellent was not having to talk. Jordan had escaped her parents who'd stared at her, faces pleated with worry. Here at least no one asked how she was.

During recreation, Jordan and Louise walked in the garden.

"Feels like I've been here for ages."

"The sign of a good retreat."

"Not talking is my new hobby."

"That's just temporary. You'll want to go back to your school, your life."

"You didn't."

"I was much, *much* older than you when I joined."

"Can I stay longer?" Jordan asked.

Their footsteps crunched gravel on the path.

"Can I come back?"

Louise smiled.

Jordan wondered if this meant yes, or maybe no, not likely. She wasn't sure. They kept walking.

"The plums are ripe," Louise pointed.

"Look at them all!" Jordan swung herself up onto a

low branch of the leafy plum tree.

She picked a smooth warm oval, dusty blue, and tossed it down to Louise. "There are tons, even more than in our alley. I'm going to need a bag. Catch!" Jordan tossed another. Touching the bark, half-hidden in the greenery, she was eleven, hiding up in the plum trees that grew in yards along the alley, climbing and picking plums with Fred.

"OK, stop! Just wait. Let me get a pail."

"I can make plum cake! I can make ten cakes!" From her perch in the branches, Jordan heard kids playing and a soccer ball thudding against the stone wall. She picked several plums and hopped down. Moving out from under the tree for a better shot, she lobbed one over, waited, and threw another. Then another. The fruit flew high over the wall.

She imagined it landing in the kids' game. She listened to excited shouts and as she prepared to toss another one, she wished she could see their reaction and whether they would catch it.

LOUISE came back with a large metal bowl, heard children shouting and paused to watch Jordan throw plums high over the wall. Not everyone had voted in favour of the girl spending a week with them. Although some cloisters rented rooms for contemplative retreat, the Carmelites of Mile End had never done so. These things didn't change overnight.

In the garden they often found items that had been flung in from outside. A shoe, a pizza box, an old tennis ball. Offering—even tossing—something from the inside out was different. This was possibly a first.

LUNA looked up.

It was like that book when it was raining meatballs. Were the nuns really throwing plums? So weird.

"Come on, Maya. Oscar!" She held out the front of her shirt and motioned her friends to do the same. They wove around bonking into each other at the spot where the other ones had splattered, necks bent, shirts out, waiting, trying not to step in plum slime. Was it over? That's it? *Shh*, she put her finger to her lips. They waited. Maya coughed.

Then, finally. Another one came sailing through the air. Luna's shirt was bigger than a baseball glove, she had a chance, a few seconds to get to the spot where she thought it was going to—

—land.

About the Author

Sarah Gilbert has been living in Mile End since 1990. Stories from her popular blog on changes in the neighbourhood were featured in various publications, including the book *Histoire du Mile End* by Yves Desjardins. Her fiction has appeared in a range of literary journals. Gilbert has worked as a freelance writer, a researcher, and a radio producer. She is a faculty member at Dawson College where she teaches literature.